The Plaza

No Frills
<<<>>>
Buffalo

Praise for **The Plaza**

"Mr. Paxton brilliantly captures the sense of despair and hopelessness that encompasses the daily lives of the citizens of Juarez. They are caught in the crossfire, with nowhere to go. They can trust no one and if they dare speak out, they are killed. Not even the innocent escape the wrath of the cartels.

We are given a glimpse of the cartel's interworking through the genuinely frightening and psychopathic personalities of some of their members. Each is driven by greed, sex, violence and power. They are chillingly sinister; amoral, corrupt and devoid of any semblance of mercy or humanity. We are provided insights to the rivalries and secret alliances that are taking place and come away realizing that the cartels are capable of anything and their influence is far reaching. Even into the Federal Police and the highest offices of government.

This is a captivating and gut-wrenching book. I highly recommend it."
- Andre Lucero, Amazon.com

"Guillermo Paxton, author of the THE PLAZA, has written an intriguing contemporary novel about the devastating drug wars in Juarez, Mexico. This modern work is filled with suspense, emotional upheaval, romantic encounters, bizarre action, and riveting ups and downs experienced by an array of diverse characters. Paxton has described a world that is rich in fascinating detail. The fact that this is a piece of fiction based on actual events witnessed by the author only makes the story more compelling and the anticipation of reading it more exciting. It is an unforgettable novel that you won't put down."
- R. Hastings, Amazon.com

"Captivating and engaging. I couldn't put it down."
- Thomas Granger Lusk, Amazon.com

"The characters felt very real to me and I cried when they cried and laughed when they did. I felt the fear they felt as the violence engulfed them and became a part of every day life, as I am sure it has become in the city of Juarez, Mexico."
-Manuela Torres, Amazon.com

"I picked this book up for an easy read and ended up reading till 3am. The vivid descriptions, character development made me both hate, love and understand the characters. Very well written."
- Paul Morin, Amazon.com

The Plaza

By Guillermo Paxton

No Frills Buffalo
<<<>>>
Buffalo NY
Nofrillsbuffalo.com

Printed in the United States of America

Paxton, Guillermo

The Plaza/ Paxton- 2nd Edition

ISBN: 978-0615626963

1. The Plaza – Crime – Fiction.   2. Mexico – New Author – No Frills – Fiction.
1. Title

No Frills Buffalo Press
119 Dorchester Buffalo, New York 14213
For More information Visit Nofrillsbuffalo.com

Dedicated to the fallen heroes, innocent victims, and dedicated journalists of Mexico and especially the city of Juarez, Mexico.

Prologue

"Hey, Jorge, you know what that is right there?"

"No, Felipe, you tell me."

"That, my friend, is *almost* a good cop."

Melendez had seen the two men standing across the street in front of his house, but he hadn't paid them any attention until they said the word "cop." Even though he wasn't currently in uniform, he was the only police officer on the entire block and in fact the whole neighborhood. Adrenalin rushed into his veins; his heart pounded in his ears. He felt the hot, August wind on his neck, and he took a deep breath. He had felt a strange feeling of apprehension since the night before, spent extra time with his two daughters and had made love to his wife more passionately than he had in years. He had even said a prayer, something he thought he had nearly forgotten how to do. He had his car keys in his hand, ready to open the door, and in just a minute more his seven year old daughter, the older of the two, would be running out to join him so he could take her to school. One more minute, and his daughter would be in danger. His sweet daughter who was quite innocent of the awful things he had done, the evil people he had worked for, and the many times he had chosen not to act when he should have while he had been a police officer for the City of Juarez, would now be in the line of fire. His hands shook violently, afraid for himself, but more afraid for his family. Why had he joined the Gente Nueva? He had told his wife that moving to Juarez would be a huge step up, but he had omitted one important detail; he was to be in service here to Chapo Guzman's mafia. He tilted his head back, then to the left, then to the right, stretching his neck, hearing it crack. He took another deep breath. Melendez made his move, reaching for the .357 he had tucked in his waist and he turned around, his tremulous hand barely able to place his finger on the trigger.

Suddenly, AK-47 bullets ripped into Melendez's chest, arms, stomach, and legs. Bullets ripped open his face and skull. They pierced into his muscles and nerves, shattering his bones. They ripped apart his intestines, his liver, his lungs, and his heart. Urine and blood ran down both legs of his pants. He was pinned, his back to the car, blood and matter flying all around him. His gun fell out of his finally still hand. The windshield of his car shattered, bullets making a sort of zigzag trail on the hood from left to right. Melendez was unrecognizable now as bullet holes replaced where his eyes, nose, and mouth had been just a few seconds before. Blood ran from the shredded body, pouring onto the cement road like spilled paint from a tilted pail. The sounds of women screaming and crying could be heard from within the Melendez home.

The man called Felipe spit. "Jorge, *now* that is a good cop." Laughing, the two men threw their AKs into the back of the white Ford Expedition they had been standing by, got in, and drove off. A woman and two young girls ran outside, screaming and crying. Neighbors poked their heads out of their doors and windows, and confirming the deadly scene was over, began to crowd around their dead neighbor. The quiet murmur of the crowd could barely be heard over the crying women. A man mentioned to someone else that they should call the police, and another bystander said not to because it wouldn't make a difference. Shortly thereafter, eight soldiers of the Mexican army arrived in a large pickup and shouted orders at the people crowded around the bloody scene who then obediently backed away. A woman covered with Melendez' blood had her arms around the torn flesh that once had been her husband and refused to let him go. The two daughters were taken away by the soldiers and put in the truck's cabin. The soldiers questioned the crowd, but everyone gave the same basic story. They had heard the shots and came out after a SUV had sped away. Being a witness or informant in Juarez was a sure way to catch a bullet.

Chapter One

Saul Saavedra had been a journalist in Juarez for the majority of his adult life. After he graduated from the local university with a degree in journalism, he started as an intern in *the Juarez Daily*, the only professional newspaper in Juarez. There were other places where, sure, he could have started out as a reporter, but they were full of horrendous, yellow journalism, graphic pictures of the dead in their perspective crime scenes, and naked girls, from the cover to the back. He wanted to be a serious reporter. After a few years of working for next to nothing, with few rewards and little hope to become a real reporter, thirty year veteran reporter Santamaria retired, leaving Saul his position at the *Juarez Daily*. At the retirement party, Saul celebrated his new position more than Santamaria's time with the paper. Knowing that he would now make a halfway decent living, he asked his girlfriend whom he had met in college to marry him the next day.

Twenty years later, Saul sat in a smoky bar waiting for an informant, not worried that he would be recognized. Part of *the Juarez Daily's* policy was to not print any of the crime reporters' pictures, ever, so he was still quite anonymous. His cell phone rang.

"What's up, babe."

"Saul, when are you coming home? It's late," said his wife Edilia.

"I know, but I'm waiting for someone, a hell of a story."

"Are you waiting for that guy that works for the mafia?"

"Yes. Now I have to go, okay?"

"Be careful my love.""

Saul hung up and put the ringer on vibrate. The informant was late, but he couldn't afford not to wait; this guy had inside information that was invaluable. A few minutes later, the informant walked in. He was tall, kind of thick in the waist, with dark hair and a dark mustache. He had a circular bald spot in the crown of his head. He wore an expensive Italian suit with equally expensive shoes. His wardrobe was easily worth more than what Saul made in half a year. Both men had today's edition of the *Juarez Daily* with them, as they had agreed to bring before the meeting so that they could recognize each other. The man smiled at Saul and sat in a booth in the back of the bar next to the jukebox. Saul stood up, paper in hand, and followed him to the booth, shaking hands with the man before sitting.

"Thanks for agreeing to meet me here. No one I know comes to this place."

Saul looked around at the almost empty bar. "I don't think anyone but you comes to this place."

The informant laughed. "No, I suppose they don't. I like your style, Saul, and I knew that I'd like you. You're a talented reporter. That's why I called you."

Saul smiled back, a warm and genuine smile that would put anyone at ease with him. "Thanks. Now, before we start, I think that it is important that we talk about our boundaries and make sure we are both clear on what can and cannot be written."

"Fair enough, but before we start with the boundaries, I need a stiff drink." He waved at the lone waitress of the bar who was busy messaging someone from her cell phone. She saw him, closed the phone and walked over to their booth.

"You like Scotch?" Saul nodded affirmatively, but he normally drank something more affordable. "Two Buchanans with mineral water." He turned to Saul for approval of his choice, and Saul nodded again.

The waitress left for the drinks and returned a few minutes later. The men drank and talked about nothing really important. Saul decided not to pressure him anymore; after all, this man had called him and would tell him whatever he was going to tell him in due time. After two more drinks, which Saul was starting to feel, the man began to talk about things more pertinent to the mafia.

"That son of a bitch president of ours, Calderon, has really screwed things up. War on drugs." The man laughed, a cynical sounding noise exiting his mouth.

"Forty god damn years the United States has been at it, and they haven't changed a thing. What in the world makes him think that he can make a difference? The United States doesn't have half the corruption that we do. They have almost unlimited funding, state of the art technology, and people who really give a shit, and yet they haven't been able to even put a dent in drug trafficking. Calderon has to be some kind of ignorant bastard to think that he can do something different here. And then he takes the stand of an all out frontal assault. Shit!"

Saul agreed wholeheartedly with the man. Prior to Calderon, the mafias in Mexico warred very little, and their executions rarely affected the general society. After he began the so-called war on drugs, the Arellano-Felix cartel was hit hard, and with their weakening, other cartels became stronger and much more audacious. The balance of crime in Mexico had been tilted. The Arellano-Felix had been the most feared cartel to ever hit Mexico, their bloody rise in the eighties setting new marks for what was known as "ruthless". When their top men were jailed or killed, two other cartels began to fight for the territory of Baja California and Sonora, The Arellano's main stronghold. El Chapo Guzman, who had been eying their territory for years, was emboldened and hit hard. He recruited many of Calderon's army that were already fighting Arellano's men, and the joined forces further weakened what remained there. There were so many losses to the Arellanos that mainstream society began to believe that Calderon had sided with El Chapo.

But the Baja California and Sonora borders were not enough for El Chapo. He wanted it all, so he sent people to recruit for him in Juarez and Reynosa, two other major drug trafficking hot spots. Meanwhile another cartel began to gain power in central Mexico, La Familia Michoacana. Most of the men in La Familia were ex-military, and they were even more ruthless than El Chapo and the Arellanos, beginning a trail of beheadings stretching from Michoacán to Tijuana. With the three major cartels and the military in constant battle, it was no coincidence that funeral homes became the fastest growing business in Mexico. With major crime rampant in the country, smaller factions of extortionists and armed robbers began to terrorize small businesses, restaurants, and mom and pop shops.

The man continued. "As you know, the Linea has been the controlling mafia in the entire state of Chihuahua. La Familia Michoacana is out now. They were losing too many people between the Linea and El Chapo. But El Chapo won't leave. He has sided with the army and that has made him very strong. His people call themselves the new people, Gente Nueva."

Saul nodded. He already knew all of this, and the look on his face surely implied it.

"Here is what you probably don't know. The Linea has set a law for all of Juarez. No one is to buy or sell drugs in Juarez any more without strict permission from one of the Captains. Everything else is being moved to the U.S. This way they can keep track of who is with them and who isn't. Anyone who doesn't follow the rules will be killed."

Saul shuddered at the implications. The drug war was bad for all of Mexico, but the killings were only part of the problem. Drug dealing, both on the street and trafficking levels, was a big part of the economy. Without the money that was spent in Mexico from the drug revenues and the many money-laundering operations, Mexico's already fragile economy would surely worsen. Furthermore, Mexico's infrastructure was not at all equipped for such a serious task.

As if he had read Saul's mind, the man continued, "You and I both know that drug money drives the Mexican economy, on local, state, and federal levels, and no one is more at fault than the gringos for that. Mexico has always been very dependent on the gringos for their buying power. My grandfather smuggled liquor to them during prohibition. Yet, they point their fingers at us bad Mexicans. And Calderon follows their demands like a dog and his master just so he can get their piddling millions to help him fight drugs." He paused and let out a sarcastic half-laugh.

"Anyway, let me tell you what we're looking at now with this law that the Linea has made. Obviously, there will be many more killings. And street dealers who actually pay attention to the law will have to find something else to do. You think that they are going to work at something legit?"

Saul shook his head. "Exactly. They are used to money, real money, not the sixty dollars a week they can earn at the local factories. And most of these guys aren't educated. Hell, I'm educated and I work for them. So imagine these guys. You know what it means?"

Saul nodded. "More robberies, more violent crimes."

"Yes. And not just that, Saul. Extortion. It has already started. Street dealers are joining forces and are hitting local businesses for protection money. It's just going to get worse. The Linea has the entire state of Chihuahua under their rule and have for more than twenty years. More cops work for them than cops that don't, if you get what I mean. The Chapo has a war on his hands here that won't be like that with the Arellanos."

"So why have you come to me about this?"

"As I said, I'm an educated person. I don't want to go into what I do or who I am. I'm sure you understand." The man waited to continue until Saul nodded that he did.

"But I wasn't always the son of a bitch that I am now. I was a law abiding, upright person. Anyway, I may be a greedy bastard, but I love Mexico. Always have. Perhaps if people see the truth about this written somewhere, they will get off their lazy asses and do something about this bullshit."

"Maybe. The government raises taxes, takes away our freedoms, and we don't do anything about it, neither individually or collectively. But I'll write it, be assured. The people of Juarez have a right to know what is really happening here. Even if they don't do anything about it."

"Right. Saul, let's drink to that." He ordered two more drinks, which Saul tried to pay for, but the man would have nothing of it.

"Thanks. What should I call you?"

"Lic." Lic was short for Licenciado or counselor.

"Okay Lic. Let's toast to the richest men in Juarez, the owners of the funeral parlors."

"And to the assassins, the busiest men in Juarez," Lic added.

Chapter Two

The faded black Fierro's driver side was smashed, and the car was partially on the median and blocking oncoming traffic in one lane. The firemen were using a steel bar to pry open the door. A man that identified himself as the driver's father was being interviewed by one of the local TV station's reporters.

"So this police detective comes barreling down the road and runs right through the red light, hitting my son." The man's face was red with anger as he pointed at the gray Dodge pickup, an unmarked vehicle used by many detectives in Juarez.

"They always do that. They barrel through red lights without any precaution, supposedly responding to an emergency. And they never catch any of the bad guys, just rush to the scene so they can put up a barricade around the dead bodies and then do nothing. Makes no sense to me. And the worst part is no one will pay for the damages! The cops will somehow make this my son's fault, you'll see!"

Saul wrote notes on his pad, silently agreeing with the man. Accidents like this happened several times a month, caused by police vehicles driving unsafely to emergencies that really weren't emergencies anymore because the victims were already dead. The impact had been so hard that the car had spun around several times and went over the median into the opposite lane of traffic.

A paramedic was inside the car, having entered through the passenger side, and was placing a neck brace on the young man, who was conscious and complaining of excruciating pain. No one in the crowd that had gathered to watch this person's suffering seemed to know why the jaws of life were not being used, and Saul heard a fireman say that they didn't have it in their unit for some reason. Saul tried to speak with the detective, but he was not talking to the media at all, and Saul was promptly waived away.

It took the firemen nearly two hours to get the victim out of the vehicle. The cop that hit him was long gone, his Dodge towed away. Saul learned from the father that the victim was twenty-one years old and a student at the state university, and he had been en route to school when the cop crashed into him. The young man was drifting in and out of consciousness as the EMTs lifted him and the gurney he was on and placed him carefully into the ambulance. The crowd disbursed, the victim's father followed the ambulance in his Ford Ranger, and another tow truck came for and took away the Fierro.

Saul left the scene, his heart heavy, but he knew who could cheer him up. And he needed a haircut anyway.

Chapter Three

Saul parked his car across the street from the barber shop that was on the corner of Zaragoza Street and Tapioca. The shop was a small room that had been converted into a fairly decent business because of its location just off a street with a lot of passing traffic. A large set of apartment buildings in a highly populated neighborhood were also nearby.

Manuel, the barber, was always busy. Saul remembered when they had met, just a few years earlier when Manuel had set up shop close to where Saul lived. Manuel had only been in Juarez for five years at that time, after having lived illegally in Colorado. He had a criminal past and had spent time in prison, but they never discussed any of that. He did such a fine job of cutting Saul's hair that when Manuel moved his shop to Zaragoza, Saul followed him even though the shop was much farther. Saul regularly gave Manuel a hard time because he always had the yellow journalistic piece of crap paper there as opposed to the *Juarez Daily*, a real paper.

"What's up, Meny?"

"I figured you'd be around pretty soon. It's been like almost three weeks since you last had your hair cut."

"Yeah. I see you still are littering the shop with piñata stuffing," Saul said, pointing to the paper called *PM*. "Just once, I'd like to see a real newspaper here."

Manuel laughed, picked up the paper, and opened it right to a centerfold model with small black stars covering her nipples and private area. "Your paper doesn't have hotties like her. Start putting babes like this in your articles, and I might actually read them while I take a dump."

"You'd have to learn to read first!"

Both men laughed and shook hands. It was ten in the morning, and Manuel had barely opened, so they were the only two in the shop. Saul sat down on the barber chair in front of the mirror. Manuel didn't ask Saul how he wanted his haircut; Saul never changed his style and Manuel knew what number on the clippers to use already. Saul wondered if he remembered that for all his regulars or just certain ones. Manuel had a plastic container that said "Sour Cream" on the counter, just under the mirror. It no longer contained sour cream but was now used as a cash register of sorts with a few fifty peso bills in it and some change.

"Meny, you aren't worried about someone robbing you?" Saul pointed with his lips at the container.

"Why?"

Manuel looked at the plastic container to which Saul was motioning with his lips. "Because of that? No, if they come to rob me, I doubt it will make a difference if the money is in plain sight or in my pocket. At least this way it is easier to get to, and I don't fill my wallet or pockets with hair."

Saul nodded. "Yeah, that makes sense. What about extortion? Do you pay protection money? I'm just curious, off the record."

"That's okay. No, I don't pay protection money. I cut the hair of some pretty bad men, heavies, and they wouldn't let that happen. And most of the youngsters that are in gangs and all that, well, I cut their hair too. They don't want a bad haircut."

"I guess no one does, really."

"Saul, the young men today are different. They are even vainer than we were at their age. Haven't you noticed the plucked eyebrows, their perfect shaves?"

"I have. Can't say I understand why these guys do their eyebrows. I always thought that was more a gay thing."

"Not anymore. These kids go out, steal, kill, sell drugs, whatever, but they make sure that when they do it, they look their best. All the newest fashion trends, cream, cologne, the works."

"Don't you ever worry that someone's going to go off on one of your clients here?"

"Of course I do. But what can I do, Saul? I can work and make a living or not. I can't exactly discriminate against the criminals. Hell, they are my best customers. Better than your cheap ass, that's for sure."

"I almost always leave you a tip!"

"Yeah. And I almost always use it to buy the *PM*."

Saul feigned anger, and both men laughed again. They talked a bit about the state of affairs in Juarez, women, and the good old days. Saul's fifteen minute haircut was stretched out for another thirty minutes, and Manuel cleaned up Saul's neck, sideburns, and behind his ears with a new razor that he took right out of the pack. Some young men came in and sat down. Saul felt a little nervous because they were obviously gangsters, but Manuel seemed to know them well. He finished with the Saul's haircut, Saul paid him, and they touched fists.

"See you in a few weeks, Meny."

"You better. I'll need another PM by then."

"Rat bastard. Learn to read first!" Saul shook his head and laughed as he left. May God protect this man, he thought. He was just getting settled into his car when a call arrived on his cell phone.

Chapter Four

"It's your dime."

"Get your butt over to Clinic Thirty-Six on Triunfo de la Republica. A man was killed there, and patients are being turned away."

"Execution?"

"It was the security guard. I don't think it was an execution, more like a murder."

"I'm on it."

Saul headed through the traffic, passing convoys of trucks packed with uniformed federal police officers armed with AR-15s. He had to go through a road block, also manned by the feds, and the cop that had him roll down his window was curt and tyrant-like, but he let Saul through without a vehicle search. He found parking a few blocks from the clinic and walked towards the building. An older, heavyset woman with dirty gray hair, wearing sweats and an apron, sold candy, gum and soft drinks out of a small stand in front of the entrance. Saul stopped and bought some gum. He introduced himself to the lady, and her eyes widened. She smiled, as if she was talking to a celebrity of some kind.

"Did you know the man that was killed?"

"Mr. Franco? Of course." Her face drooped into a sincere expression of sadness. "Such a nice man. A good man. He's been a security guard at night here for like ten years, maybe sixty years old, can't understand why they had to kill him. What could he have possibly done to deserve that?"

"What does anyone do to deserve death in this city? He might have stopped a thief, or he could have just looked at someone the wrong way. Who knows?" Saul shook his head, and then he thanked the woman. He tried to enter the building with his press credentials, but he was stopped by a federal policeman in his dark blue uniform and a ski mask.

"No one goes in."

"What can you tell me about the-"

"Nothing. You can talk to the media relations officer later like everyone else."

Saul raised his eyebrows and pursed his lips. "Thanks for nothing." He turned around and walked away, hearing a smug laugh coming from the policeman that had barred his entrance. *No problem, I'll just head over to the back of the building and talk to one of the nurses or doctors who are outside on a smoke break.*

Saul approached a tall, skinny man in a nurse's uniform that was smoking alone. "How's it going?"

"Good." The man looked at the press credentials that hung off of Saul's neck and nodded. "You here about the night watchman?"

"Yeah."

The man offered Saul a cigarette. Saul accepted it, pulled one out of the pack, and let the other man light it for him. Saul inhaled and stopped a cough in his throat. He didn't smoke very often, usually just when he wanted to get information from a smoker.

"Thanks," he said, exhaling smoke as he spoke, his taste buds angry at the smoke emissions entering their cavity.

"Too bad, killing a person for a big screen TV."

Saul nodded as if he already knew the information.

"So did you hear who they think did it?"

Saul shook his head no. The nurse, apparently pleased that he had information that Saul did not have, was eager to share details with him.

"Well, apparently a young man that was working with him has disappeared. At first, they thought that he might have been abducted, but now the cops think that he was the one who did it."

"Really? Wow, wish you knew the kid's name."

The nurse smiled. "Who said that I didn't?"

Saul knew that going to see the suspect murderer at his home unarmed and without company was a bad idea, but he was going to do it anyway. The security company had been kind enough to give him the address of the missing employee. At the apartment complex, he knocked on the door that had the number fifteen painted on it in green, block letters. A young man's voice answered.

"Who is it?" It was the voice of a scared person trying to sound tough.

"This is Saul, Jeremy. I'm a reporter with the *Juarez Daily*, and I know what happened at the hospital. I just came over to get your side of the story before you are picked up by the cops and they tell me something completely different. What do you say?" Saul could see movement through the peephole in the door, and he lifted his reporter's credentials up high so that they would be easily seen.

Jeremy opened the door. He had a black scythe tattooed on his neck, and he wore black eyeliner around his eyes. "Come on in."

"So you don't plan to hide from the cops?"

"No, I would just get caught later."

Saul nodded. "So what happened?"

Jeremy shook his head and sat down on a dirty black couch. Besides the TV, the couch was the only other furniture in the small living room. It looked as if the couch doubled as a bed; a sheet and pillow with dark stains on it were at the end of it.

"Old man was always giving me shit about being too young for a job like this, for my tattoos, my eyebrows, my earrings, all the time, constantly. I got sick of it. I beat him down. He pulled out his baton. I stabbed him. I didn't mean to kill him. I promise. Really, it just got ahead of me."

"So you stole a big screen TV?"

Jeremy looked at him inquisitively, not quite comprehending the question. "TV?"

"They said you took a big screen TV after you killed Mr. Franco."

"I didn't. How would I take it? I don't even have a car. The cops probably took it and are blaming me."

Saul nodded affirmatively at the possibility. "Don't worry; I'll make sure that goes in my article too."

A loud crashing sound erupted from the door as it was busted open, splinters and paint chips flying everywhere. The cops were yelling and pointing AR-15s at Saul and Jeremy. Saul got down to the floor, and when the cop finished searching and handcuffing him, Saul asked for them to kindly look at the credentials hanging from his neck. Alongside Jeremy, the cops gave Saul a free trip to the processing center where he was imprisoned for at least a few hours in a twenty by twenty cell with ten other men. When he was finally released to the paper's editor, Michelle, the adrenaline rush and subsequent drop from the self-induced high had taken its toll. He arrived at the *Juarez Daily* a fraction of the man that had arrived to work in the morning. He spent several hours writing his stories that were to be ready for tomorrow's edition of the paper, catching mistake after grammatical mistake that his exhausted mind kept making, further exasperating the process.

When he got home, it was past nine, and dinner had to be warmed up. Edilia was in pajamas and the girls were sleepy. He talked very little as the events of the day still weighed heavily upon him. He apologized to his family and told them that it had been a difficult day. He didn't even feel like making love to Edilia, which was rare, and she fell asleep soon after they went to bed.

Exhausted as he was, sleep was an ever more elusive function for Saul as the situation in Juarez progressively worsened. He was incredibly tired, but his mind recalled the events of the day many times over. He also pondered his writing, and he ended up critiquing his work harshly, admonishing himself for his mediocre efforts.

Remembering his meeting with the mafia lawyer informant, Saul wondered about his family's safety and about his friends who had fled Juarez because of the extortion. That train of thought led him to wonder who would be his new family doctor now that his doctor of more than twenty years had left too.

He remembered the call from Mario Olivera, the man who had brought both of his daughters into the world. He recalled the man's hands shaking and his nervous behavior that stood out quite differently from his usually calm and jovial self. He had related to Saul how three armed men had walked into his clinic and demanded five hundred dollars a week, or they would have to end his life. Mario's clinic maybe generated that much money a week, and after he paid his nurses and other expenses, little remained. Saul knew Mario to be a very modest doctor, and that kind of money would have quickly bankrupted him. Mario closed the doors to the clinic the same day and never looked back, and Saul had not yet even started looking for another doctor.

Sleep finally fell upon Saul, but it was restless and violent. When he finally fell into a deep sleep, it was time to get up again. The alarm blasted its way into his dreams, and he reluctantly opened his eyes and willed his body to get up.

His cell phone rang while he was showering. Edilia took him the phone.

"Babe, your phone," she said.

He stuck his arm out from behind the shower curtain and dried his hand on a towel; then he took it from Edilia.

"Thanks," he told her. He opened the cell phone and answered.

"Remember the kid from the car accident yesterday?" his editor asked.

"Yeah..."

"He died last night due to complications."

"Okay. I'll write it. Thanks. See you at ten for the meeting."

Saul didn't know the young man, but he still felt saddened by the news. He remembered the father complaining about how the cops would make this his son's fault, about who would pay for damages and medical bills, not even considering the idea that his son might not survive. The young man had been talking to the paramedics when Saul had last seen him boarding the ambulance. He had seemed very alive, and while he was hurt, he was certainly not in that grave of condition.

Saul got ready for work and went downstairs, still amazed about how life could drastically change in a mere instance. Edilia was at the table having coffee. She got up and prepared him a cup as well. Saul graciously accepted the coffee, taking a drink like a diver would breathe his first breath of air after having been under water.

"Breakfast?"

"I lost my appetite."

Edilia shook her head. "That bad, huh?"

"Yeah. That bad. Going to be a long day," extending the word "long" for emphasis. Edilia shook her head again and smiled.

"Don't let the job eat you alive, honey. Remember your family is first; the job is second. And really, you don't have to take on the pain of the people that you are reporting."

Saul gave a half smile. "Easier said than done. I can't help but to be empathetic with these people."

"I know. I think it is why you are such a good reporter. That's part of it, at least. Now make sure you have some energy tonight for me when you get home. I don't want a repeat of last night."

Saul smiled, and his face flushed at his wife's hint at his lack of sexual appetite. "You're on."

He drove to the office, quickly identifying possible escape routes in case of a firefight at every stop like usual. He had been at the office just long enough to pour himself a coffee when he got a call on his cell phone. His police informant, a police dispatcher that Saul paid with small gifts and occasional cash, told him of a new crime scene. Saul quickly finished his coffee in a few swallows, gathered up his belongings, and left immediately for the action.

Chapter Five

As Saul approached the scene, the passengers had emptied the bus. Women were crying and men were visibly shaken. The bus was a typical public transportation bus, but it was painted red and white. It was probably from the United States dating to the late seventies or early eighties. On the rear of the bus, block letters were painted in yellow that read "In Loving Memory, El Chucky."

Three armed men had boarded the bus and one shot one of the passengers in the head. Crime was so rampant, and almost never punished, that criminals did not care who witnessed their terrible acts, even a busload of passengers. The woman that had been sitting beside the victim was covered in his blood, and she was still shaking and crying while a city police officer attempted to calm her. Saul was impressed with the officer's compassion; so many of them were emotionally detached, empathy alien to their character. The officer was gentle and kind with his words, and eventually he calmed her down enough that she could describe the incident. She wouldn't give him any descriptions of the shooters though, and Saul really didn't expect her to. Only the most brave people, or ignorant, would give information to the police in any manner other than anonymously.

Saul spent the entire day covering homicides to include two men at a restaurant, a married couple outside of a shopping center, and some young men who were executed while playing soccer. Saul wrote his articles and drove home. He normally played the radio in the car, but today, he didn't want any noise. He felt as if his brain was already full of noise. As usual, he looked for escape routes at every stoplight and remained vigilant for attacks, either on him or on others. He was careful to not take a direct route back home. He stopped a few blocks before the turn to his street to ensure he had not been followed. Relieved that he had not, he finally arrived home. *This is no way to live,* Saul thought. *There is not one moment, not one second that I can relax outside of my home.*

Saul kissed Edilia. He played with the girls, transforming himself into a human bull; the girls playing cowgirls while he gently bucked them off his back. After about ten minutes, Saul was sweating and found himself somewhat out of breath. Edilia smiled.

"Someone needs to get in shape."

"Yeah, I can fit that in somewhere between sleeping for five hours and using the bathroom in the morning."

"I'm just saying..."

They ate dinner. Saul did his best to make entertaining conversation that had nothing to do with the day's horrific events. After dinner, they drove to Borunda Park to eat ice cream bars. The park, over fifty years old, was part of Saul's earliest childhood memories, as his parents used to take him there to eat hot dogs and play on the rides. He and Edilia even married in the kiosk at the center of the park. It was Juarez's answer to a smaller and quainter Coney Island. The girls had strawberry ice cream bars while Edilia and Saul had Mexican corn on the cob, a corn that is not sweet, covered in butter, lime, and chile, and served on a stick or in a cup. Saul reminisced to when he was seven years old. Back then, Juarez was a very different city.

Saul and his parents lived close to Borunda, maybe half a mile from downtown Juarez. The neighborhood, with newly paved and clean streets, was an upper-middle class area with residents who were primarily born and reared in Juarez. The park was always full during the afternoon and evenings when the weather was warm, and Saul's parents would take him every Sunday after mass. He always looked forward to Sunday, although he could do without mass, and was always on his best behavior on Saturday so not to miss Sunday's outing.

Saul's father, an attorney, was of medium height and medium build, and his hair line receded almost to the top of his head. He was a great orator, and he would tell interesting stories of people from the Bible after church, explaining the stories without just reciting the verses outright as the priest did during the sermon. People often said he would have been a great preacher. After church they would often frequent restaurants, somewhere downtown, usually on the strip of road that led right across the border to the United States. Occasionally, they would even go to El Paso to eat, always a great treat for Saul; he enjoyed observing the gringos speak their language, the way they wore their clothes, and the subtle differences in the cultures. Many of the people from El Paso were Chicanos, Americans of Mexican descent, and they spoke a strange mix of English and Spanish. Whether they went to El Paso or stayed in Juarez, though, they inevitably ended up in Borunda.

"Did you hear a word I said?"

Saul blushed. "Sorry, dear, I'm afraid I was far away."

"No kidding. Better not have been another woman." She smiled.

"You know that the only competition you have is Lucero, and she is still married." Saul always mentioned the Mexican actress whenever his wife pretended to be jealous. He knew she really wasn't worried; Saul couldn't have found a more beautiful woman, inside and out, if he lived another thousand years, and he made sure that she knew he felt that way. Besides, his chances with Lucero were probably no better than his chances with the Queen of England.

"Well, that Jezebel better not ever get any bright ideas. As I was saying, it is getting late. We should go."

Saul frowned. It was July, the girls were on vacation from school, and it was barely 8:30 P.M. But Edilia was right. Times had changed, and the possibility of their car getting broken in to, or worse yet, their getting mugged, only increased with each hour. He called for his daughters, and they walked to the car as the girls whined about going home early. It was just another small consequence of the crime in Juarez that hurt Saul; his daughters would never know the same peace and security that he and Edilia had experienced years before in the same city. For the girls, rampant crime and murder was normal, even though Saul often made it a point to talk to them about the fact that it was not.

After loading into the car, Saul carefully maneuvered out of the parallel parking space he had done so expertly when they had arrived. He rolled down the window as a lady approached in her mid-fifties with an orange traffic vest that had been watching the car. Saul fished for ten pesos from his unused ashtray and handed it to her. He didn't give money to beggars, but the people that watched his car were not beggars at all; it was a truly viable service to provide a watchful eye over vehicles in this crime rampant city.

Saul and his family laughed and talked as they drove back to their home. For just a moment, it seemed as if they didn't really live in a war zone.

Chapter Six

Felipe took one final drag of his Marlboro, holding the smoke in his lungs and then let it escape slowly from his mouth and nose. A whore he solicited the night before was still in the bed. She didn't appear as attractive to him as she had the night before when he was drunk.

He looked at himself in the mirror. The face that peered back at him was haggard and unshaven. He had dark circles under his eyes. He wasn't much to look at, and he knew it. His nose and teeth were crooked, his ears too big, and his brown eyes were too small. He had scars from acne all over his face and back. He was thin, but it wasn't from exercise; it was just his genetic physical build. The only positive attribute he possessed was his penis; he had been told ever since he was a child that he was well-endowed. Disgusted, he quit looking at himself in the mirror.

"Hi love, why don't you come back to bed? What's the matter? Can't sleep?"

"Not while you're here. Get the fuck out. I already paid you, anyway."

"Oh, how rude!"

"Just get out, or I'll put a bullet between your eyes." He placed his hand on the .45 pistol he had on the dresser.

The woman quickly got out of bed without saying another word. She dressed, putting on her blouse first, then her skirt, and finally, her shoes. She couldn't seem to find her panties, but after Felipe's threat, she apparently decided that panties weren't really all that necessary, and she opened the door and left.

Felipe lay down, and he went to sleep almost immediately. However, his rest wasn't a deep and peaceful sleep; it never was for Felipe. His dreams were filled with the dead people he had killed, mostly men, and he would recount his victims from his very first murder to the most recent. The victims haunted him, ruining his would-be rest. They pointed accusing fingers at him and mouthed silent words. Their bodies were rotting, some more than others, and their faces showed varied states of decomposition. Soon, all the victims surrounded Felipe and retaliated. They smothered him, making it impossible to scream, or even to breathe. He woke up.

The bed was soaked with sweat. His head throbbed, and he grabbed the bottle of tequila next to the bed, drinking it thirstily. He placed the bottle back on the nightstand and replaced the cap with his free hand. He rose from the bed and took a shower. He shaved meticulously to ensure his face was as smooth as possible except for his thick, graying mustache which he trimmed. Likewise, he brushed his crooked, cigarette-stained yellow teeth and used mouthwash to rinse. As usual, he dressed in his black Wrangler jeans, black ostrich skin boots, and his black button down western shirt. He put on his gold necklace with a miniature gold AK-47. He poured tequila from his bedside bottle into a small, tin cantina and stuck it in his shirt. After tucking his .45 pistol between the small of his back and his pants, Felipe put on his expensive black Resistol cowboy hat, inspected himself in the mirror, and laughed. *El gato negro*, the black cat, he thought, and he laughed out loud again. Felipe left the motel.

It was six in the morning. La Choza was open twenty four hours, and they served great menudo. Felipe drove to one of their several locations, smoking another Marlboro as he did. When he arrived, he parked, and put out the cigarette. He stepped out of his new Dodge pickup, shut the door, and locked the vehicle. The alarm sounded two sharp beeps, alerting him that the truck was locked and that the alarm was activated. After entering the small restaurant, he sat down at a smaller table that was set for two people. The waitress came over to the table.

"Can I take your order?"

"Large menudo and coffee."

"OK."

Felipe refused to eat menudo anywhere else but La Choza. Not only was it just the right taste, but they also ran a very clean restaurant. He watched the waitress walk away and estimated she was all of maybe five feet, ninety pounds. He noticed her round ass and full breasts. Satisfied, he pulled out the cantina with tequila, opened it, and took a long drink. He replaced the twist cap, and placed it back in his shirt. The short waitress returned with his order, leaving the menudo, coffee, chili, chopped onions, and oregano. He grabbed a handful of the chopped onions and dumped them into the soupy concoction of beef tripe and maize. Needing additional flavor, he took the salt shaker that held the red chili powder and shook it vigorously over the menudo. The waitress returned and placed toasted bakery bread with butter in a bread basket on the table.

Relaxed, Felipe ate his menudo and drank his coffee. He lit another cigarette, took a deep drag, and exhaled. Someone coughing called to the waitress. A moment later, she appeared at the table again.

"Anything else I can bring you, sir? Your check?"

"No. Bring me more coffee."

She frowned. "Okay, but the couple over there is complaining about your smoking, and with the new federal law that-" Felipe interrupted her.

"What couple? Show me." She pointed at a couple seated a few tables down.

"Go get me the coffee, and don't worry about it; they won't have any more complaints."

Felipe slipped the pistol from the small of his back to his waist. He stood and walked over to the table of the complaining couple. As he stood in front of them, he smoked, without saying anything. The woman began to force a cough as she alternated between looking at her husband and Felipe. Felipe stood, saying nothing, while continually blowing his smoke at the couple. Finally, the man cleared his throat to speak.

"Sir, the law says no smoking in public areas, and my wife has asthma. Would you mind putting it out?"

Felipe moved very close to the man's ear as if he were going to whisper something.

"Yes I would. Tell me now, what does your fucking law say about guns?" he said very quietly, showing them the gun in his waist.

"Um, ne-never mind," the man stuttered. "We were just leaving."

The couple began to get out of their seats. Felipe motioned with his hand for them to sit back down, and he shook his head. They obeyed Felipe's instructions, and he walked back to his table. His coffee was already there, the steam rising from the cup. When he finished, he left enough money to cover both the bill and a decent tip. He left without hurry, got in his Dodge pickup, and drove to his meeting with Silva.

Chapter Seven

Felipe sat in the large, luxurious office of the mafia lawyer, Heliodoro Silva. Silva was a notary, a lawyer for both civil and criminal cases, and an immigration specialist. He did everything for the highest ranking members of the local controlling mafia known as La Linea, or "The Line. As a notary, he helped them buy and sell properties. Silva's brother was the state's highest legal authority; he was in charge of both the investigative and judicial departments. Silva wore very expensive slacks and shirts, and his shoes were valued more than the average Mexican citizen's annual salary. Felipe didn't care for Silva. He thought of him as a snob, pretentious, and condescending. Unfortunately, if he wanted to get paid, he had no choice but to do business with Silva.

"Felipe, every day more of Chapo's people are arriving. They are actively recruiting from the general populace and from the police, like your last mark. This is going to be a real war. I suggest you take a side. Well, El Jefe does, anyway. He promises you a high position in the organization."

Felipe shifted in the seat, sinking a bit into the plush cushion with a black, leather exterior. He knew that Silva was referring to the Gente Nueva, the new people, the cartel run by El Chapo Guzman. Gente Nueva was attempting to assume control of the Chihuahua territory, run by La Linea for as long as Felipe knew about the mafia. El Jefe, the boss, wanted Felipe to work exclusively for La Linea, and he had been soliciting Felipe's commitment for the last five years. Felipe almost always worked for La Linea, but he really didn't want to be associated with just a single cartel as it would automatically designate him an enemy of other cartels. At the same time, the Gente Nueva were murdering anyone even suspected to be a part of La Linea. Therefore, he was a part of them even if he didn't want to be. He could use the back up. It was something to which he had given much consideration long before this meeting, and he had already made his decision.

"Tell the Jefe that I accept." Silva looked surprised. "He's right; it is going to be an all out war."

Silva recovered quickly. "That will make El Jefe very happy. Now, on to new business. Calderon is sending five thousand soldiers to Juarez. El Jefe already offered one of the top men, Captain Garza, a position, but he refused. Garza El Jefe wants this kill to be very public and messy. We need to demoralize the soldiers and make Garza an example at the same time. Here is his information." Silva pushed a file across the desk towards Felipe.

Silva then put a brown paper bag with what appeared to be money inside it on the desk, and he also pushed it halfway towards Felipe. "Twenty thousand dollars upon completion. Five thousand are in this bag." It was the customary way Silva paid him.

Felipe nodded, rose, and left the office. He got into his truck and shut the door. Eager for his assignment, he opened the file and perused several photos of the Captain and his family which included leaving his kids at school and at the bowling alley. The address of the Captain's home and his kids' schools were written on the backs of the photos. Because he was a military captain, Felipe would have to be deliberate and very careful. He could easily be apprehended and made an example by the Mexican government. Felipe reasoned that he would have to conduct surveillance and determine where the Captain was most vulnerable.

Felipe slipped his keys in the ignition, turned the key, put the truck in reverse, and drove to the Captain's address, parking just a few houses down. He shut the truck off. There didn't appear to be anyone at the Captain's residence. Felipe lit a Marlboro, deeply breathing in the smoke. He rolled down his window halfway, exhaled, and the smoke slowly exited into the open air. After a couple of minutes, Felipe stiffened when a Hummer filled with soldiers passed by. He relaxed when he realized that they were only conducting a routine patrol. As they paused in front of the Captain's house, the soldier in the passenger seat wrote on a small notepad. After the soldiers passed, Felipe started the truck and went to the school where the Captain's children attended classes.

Felipe didn't care for the school area either. He assessed that there was too much movement and too many soldiers passing by. The academy was expensive, and it appeared that there was probably continual security on the premises.

Next, Felipe drove to the bowling alley. "Every Friday" was written on the back of the photo, presumably indicating how often the Captain frequented the establishment. The bowling alley was on a corner with three main roads providing access. Felipe imagined himself and his cousin pulling to the side of one of the roads adjacent to the parking lot, walking in between the parked cars, entering the building, and pulling out their .45s and blowing the Captain away.

Felipe then imagined himself and his cousin exiting the building and sprinting back to the truck only to find a police car parked behind it. He assessed they would have to park in the bowling alley's parking area instead. However, this created another problem; it was a pay to park area, and there was only one entrance and one exit. In this case, they would have to jump the curb to escape. He changed the scene in his mind again by parking next to the entrance while leaving the truck running. After they murdered the Captain, they would run out and Felipe would jump in the driver's seat. Ready to speed away, several of the Captain's men would also run after them, shooting out the tires of Felipe's Dodge pickup. The Captain's men would also shoot at the back window of his truck, and when the window shattered, Felipe and his cousin would be dead. He determined they would need more people. But this would definitely be the optimal place; the access to three major roads from the parking lot in a very public place would make a "statement" that was loud and clear.

Felipe drew a rough sketch of the bowling alley and its surroundings. He would have to study the place on a Friday night to determine the amount of traffic and people in the area. They would have to wear masks. Felipe placed the sketch into the file that he had been given, and then he phoned his cousin.

"Meet me at Los Canarios. How long before you get there?"

"Fifteen minutes."

Felipe drove to Los Canarios, a small restaurant that served only tacos and flautas. The flautas were served with cream, avocado, tomato and onion, and the best red chili sauce that Felipe had ever eaten. He waited outside until his cousin arrived. They entered together, without saying a word, and they sat in a back corner. Felipe ordered for both of them, two orders of flautas and two beers. The beers were served first, and they drank them before the flautas were served and then ordered two more. They drank beer, ate flautas, and drank more beer. When they had finished, the waiter cleared the table and wiped it down at Felipe's request. Felipe then removed his sketch from the file, laid it on the table and then he gave the picture of the Captain to his cousin.

"We'll need two more guys. One will be the driver, and the other will stay in the back of the pickup, watching our backs. He'll have an AK. You and I will carry .45s."

"Sounds good. Who you going to use?"

"We'll pick up a few gangsters from the Aztecas. A couple of guys I've used for other jobs. "

Felipe's cousin nodded. They ordered two more beers.

Chapter Eight

Captain Garza had always wanted to be a soldier for as long as he could remember. He remembered that even as a kid his skin would get goose bumps when he heard the national anthem. Now when he heard those notes, his chest would fill with pride, and others would say that it seemed as if he would even be glowing. Garza never had the notion of immigrating to the United States for better pay or an easier way of life. Instead, he preferred to better his own country. From his viewpoint, there was no better way to improve his country than to rid it of the drug traffickers that poisoned it, filling Mexico's children with drugs and false hopes of easy money. When the mafia offered him a regular stipend just for him to look the other way, he took great offense. As a result, they threatened him with anonymous texts and some spray-painted messages on walls around the city. When the General talked to him seriously about whether or not he wanted to transfer out of Juarez, Garza had told the General that no cowardly messages from the mafia would detain him, and if necessary, he would gladly give his life for Mexico.

A young man stood in front of Garza's desk, a sharp salute awaiting a response. Garza saluted back. "At ease, Lieutenant. Is your report ready?"

"Yes sir. We captured two men; we believe them to be mid-level leaders of La Linea, with three hundred kilos of marijuana, three grenades, ten assault rifles, and three handguns. Three hundred and seventy-five cartridges of distinct calibers."

"Was that in the rich neighborhood we had received the tip from?"

"Yes sir. The tip was good."

"Excellent. Any casualties?"

"Three on the enemy's side, two dead, one in the hospital. None on our side."

Garza smiled. Knowing that he had trained his men well, he remembered his last speech to them. "Always remember, men, you represent the Mexican government in its purest form, free of politics and corruption. Your number one job is to stay alive."

"Anything else, Lieutenant?"

"No sir." The Lieutenant placed a file onto Garza's desk. "My report is here, including photographs of the scene and the government's enemies that have been captured, as well as the dead."

"Excellent job, Lieutenant. I expect to see you tonight at the bowling alley and plan to buy you several pitchers of beer."

The man saluted, obviously pleased with the Captain's praise. "Yes sir! I'll be there. The only thing that could prevent my presence is my own death, and even in that case, I doubt that death could stop me from having a beer bought for me by my esteemed captain."

Garza laughed and saluted back. "So be it, Jose. You're dismissed." He picked up his phone and called his wife.

"You and the kids meet me at the bowling alley at six sharp, my love."

"We wouldn't miss it for the world. I love you."

Chapter Nine

"You ready?"

Felipe's cousin took a deep breath before answering Felipe. "Yeah. Ready."

Felipe and his cousin checked their pistols one more time, Felipe's .45 and Juan's .40 cal. Seeing that they were indeed ready, Felipe motioned to Mr. Fresa and Sad Face.

Mr. Fresa was a strange nickname for anyone in the mafia, but it was appropriate for him. He was all of twenty-five years, and his hair stood up with the hardest gel in existence. He wore a pair of designer jeans with a matching shirt and brown leather shoes. If he walked into a bar full of rich, Mexican preppies (or Fresas), he would fit right in except for the fact that Mr. Fresa carried a 9mm and would kill you for inadvertently bumping into him and not excusing yourself.

Mr. Fresa turned the ignition key and put the recently stolen truck into gear. They drove into the bowling alley's parking lot, paid the parking ticket, and drove right up to the glass front doors. The driver, Felipe, and his cousin all donned masks. Mr. Fresa had one of Mexican president Calderon, Felipe of a pig, and his cousin of an ex-president, Salinas. Sad Face in the back did not need a mask since his "day job" was as a street clown and his face was painted in a perpetual clown frown. Felipe told him that he was just going to be their back up and that his job was to kill anyone that ran out of the bowling alley that wasn't part of their team. Felipe doubted anyone would really be able to recognize him. Felipe and his cousin jumped out of the truck with their weapons in hand ready to fire.

After opening the doors, Felipe and his accomplices walked with purpose into the bowling alley. Felipe spotted the target and motioned to his cousin, and they converged upon Garza. If people saw the masked men with guns in hand, they acted as if they did not. Felipe raised his gun and shot the Captain as he turned around; his smile was wiped away from his face forever. Felipe's .45 released the first bullet from a distance of about six feet, entering his chest. Blood escaped from the entrance wound, and the Captain crashed backwards into a table and chairs from the force of the bullet. Felipe discharged three more rounds into the chest of the Captain as he was falling to the floor.

Felipe's cousin shot another man near the Captain who was reaching for a handgun from a shoulder holster. Blood also squirted out of his neck with beat of each pulse where the bullet had penetrated. As a second bullet entered his skull, blood and brain matter sprayed Garza's terrified family nearby.

A young boy screamed. Various women and a few men also began to scream. People were running frantically to escape the scene of carnage that Felipe and his cousin had raged upon the bowling alley. A woman ran to Garza's side, and she glared hatefully at Felipe. A large man ran into a pregnant woman who was also running toward the exit, knocking her down to the ground. He didn't even look back as another man helped her up. When the large man opened the glass doors of the bowling alley and ran out, Sad Face fell back into the glass doors, breaking them, with glass shards dispersing everywhere.

Others who had thought about exiting changed their minds and searched for cover as Felipe and his cousin ran out of the bowling alley and jumped into the truck, the clown covering them with fire from the bed of the pickup. Mr. Fresa floored the gas pedal, and the tires squealed desperately on the pavement. The pickup jumped the curb as planned and they sped off.

The road leaving the bowling alley had no exits for approximately two kilometers. It was the moment in their plan that Felipe knew they were most susceptible to get caught. Felipe yelled at Mr. Fresa to hurry, and he began swerving in and out of lanes, avoiding the cars that would not yield when he honked repeatedly. The few minutes that passed seemed like an eternity to Felipe and his accomplices, but a sense of relief came over them as they followed the road to a final curve that brought them to a stoplight. They would now be able to enter the residential area and disappear into the labyrinth of roads that the sprawling city with unplanned growth provided.

As they turned into the residential area, a traffic cop saw the wanted pickup and turned his motorcycle around in pursuit. Felipe opened the middle window of the truck's cabin to talk to the guy in the back, but Sad Face was already aiming his AK-47 at the traffic cop. The cop, seeing the weapon, hit the brakes hard, turning into the curb of the road, but it was too late. The bullets ripped into the ground around him, finally finding him and his motorcycle. He didn't even have time to grab his sidearm. Felipe smiled and slid the window shut.

Mr. Fresa made a series of turns to avoid those that may have been following them, and they parked behind Felipe's pickup which had been pre-positioned earlier. Mr. Fresa left the keys in the ignition of the getaway pickup, and the men, except for Sad Face, got out of the pickup, left their masks behind, and then boarded Felipe's truck. Sad Face doused the stolen truck with gas, particularly the cabin, lit a match, and he threw it into the truck. The truck exploded into flames, and he hurriedly got into the back of Felipe's pickup.

Felipe drove this time and did so calmly so as to avoid suspicion. After arriving at the safe house which they had rented a few days earlier, Felipe parked his truck in the back yard. Mr. Fresa's and the clown-faced man's cars were already parked there. The men exited the truck and entered the house through the back door. A cooler and some plastic chairs were the only things that occupied the otherwise empty home. Felipe opened the cooler and removed iced cold bottles of beer, handing one to each man. The clown opened his with his teeth, Mr. Fresa with the bottle opener that he had on his keychain. Mr. Fresa offered to open Felipe and his cousin's beers, and they accepted.

Felipe drank his beer and smiled. "Good job," he told the men.

Minutes later, the noise of a helicopter approaching above could be heard, and the men were tense until the sound faded away again. They laughed and crashed their beer bottles together, yelling "salud."

The men drank beer for several hours. Sad Face went to the bathroom, and after a while, he returned with a clean face. Felipe thought he looked better with his face painted and told him so. The other men laughed, but he and Felipe did not. When the other men stopped laughing, feeling the tension, Felipe and the other man laughed, even harder than the other two had a moment before. Then they all laughed again.

Chapter Ten

"I don't believe that bullshit that people choose their own parents...have you ever heard that?"

The prison psychologist thought about it for a moment, and then frowning, said, "No, I don't believe I have, Juan." He was dressed in a pair of brown slacks and a blue button down shirt with no tie for safety reasons.

"Yeah, one of my ex-girlfriends told me this shit, you know, that when you are born you choose your own parents. Something about it being harder to get into heaven when you choose good parents. I used to think about that. It bothered me. I don't know, but it seems like bullshit to me."

"Why did it bother you?"

"Because no one in their right mind would ever have picked the parents I had. No one. Not even for an easier ticket into heaven. Hell, not even for a free ticket to heaven. Fuck that."

"You never have spoken to me about them."

"And I ain't gonna start, Doc."

"Okay then. So tell me what your plans are when you get out."

Juan Del Rio smiled, not a wide grin, but a half smile that barely lifted on one corner of his lips. That was the most of a smile that anyone would ever see on his face. He eased back into his chair, his broad chest and shoulders relaxing slightly. He always looked ready to fight, even in his semi relaxed position, which was a consequence of having spent many years in gangs and prison. His head was clean shaven, and his prison muscles were very evident under the plain white t-shirt he wore.

"Well, you see, I made a deal with the prosecution. They agreed to lower my sentence if I voluntarily deport myself back to Mexico."

"But you've lived almost your entire life in the United States."

"Yeah, and most of my adult life in the pinta. When I was sixteen and got tried as an adult, I spent seven years in jail. I got out, and I couldn't find a fucking job. No one would even give me the time of day. I didn't have to tell anyone I was a con, though, because they already knew."

Juan pointed at his teardrop tattoos running from the corner of his right eye, then the one on his neck, the number thirteen in Roman numerals.

"It is obvious. Even if I didn't have these, I did my best Doc, really. I didn't want to fucking go back inside for nothing. I fucking hated being locked up. I knew guys that actually liked that shit, can you believe that? They said it was easier inside, with your three squares, tele, fucking library, drugs as needed. I'm thirty-five now. Spent the last sixteen years in jail. Mexico may be my last shot. At least there I'll have a clean slate."

After years of working with Chicanos in prison, the doctor followed the jargon fine, knowing that pinta meant prison and tele was short for television. "So where do you plan to go?"

"Ciudad Juarez."

"I see that place on TV all the time. Very violent place. It is dangerous. Are you sure you want to go there?"

"Shit Doc, *I'm* dangerous. We're perfect for each other."

Chapter Eleven

The weeks that followed prior to Juan's release seemingly dragged on longer than the last three years he had spent in prison. But the day finally arrived, and he was driven to the border. After assisting Juan out of the transport van, the deputies removed his handcuffs. They were near the bridge that connected El Paso, Texas with Ciudad Juarez, Mexico. After they stepped away from him, Juan stretched his arms and legs and moved his head around in a circle; it had been a long ride. He was a bridge away from becoming a completely free man to start a new life without a prison record always haunting him. He knew it wouldn't be easy, but the price of freedom was always high. Others before him had paid a higher price.

"There you go, con, your new home. It's a fucking jungle over there. Perfect for you."

Juan's hands clenched into fists, and his half-smile became a grimace, but he did not respond. He vowed not to return to prison ever again. He'd rather be dead. He picked up the duffel bag that had three changes of clothes, all of Juan's worldly possessions, and began walking the trail that led to the bridge, enclosed by a chain link fence. The deputies had no reason to worry because he had no intentions of trying to escape. If he escaped, he would be hunted like an animal until caught and would never get out of jail again. He walked quickly up the bridge, pausing for a moment at the sign that marked the imaginary line that was known as the border. He thought about taking a piss right on the sign, but he decided against it and continued moving on. He then turned around to find the deputies still watching him. He gave them a one finger salute, and they returned it in the same fashion. He turned back towards Mexico and continued walking.

Juan could almost taste freedom as it seemed to permeate from the soil of Mexico. People always talked about the United States as a place people went to be free, but it was nothing like Mexico. There were people set up on every corner, all along the street, selling food, gum, cigarettes, flavored waters and other sundry items. A young girl, barely eighteen if that, tried to convince him to go into the bar that she stood in front of, Tito's. Beggars, children, and old people were everywhere. There were some cops all in a group talking to some whores. A man approached and told Juan that he could get him anything he needed - drugs, girls, boys, whatever. *What a great place it indeed*! Juan thought.

Juan didn't have a dime to his name. He walked into a small store that also rented telephone time and sat down at a booth. He remembered as a kid his mom calling people from a place like this one. In poor Spanish, he asked how to dial the United States and a middle age man answered him.

"Zero, zero, then the number."

Juan dialed zero, zero, one and the number. A man named Crazy answered.

"Yeah, it's your dime mother fucker."

"It's me, Crazy."

"Fuck," Crazy said, drawing out the word for several seconds, "How'd you get out? Did you escape?"

"No, man, I made a deal with the fuckin´ DA, and they let me out as long as I deported myself. Something about no longer being a burden on the tax payers."

"No shit? Deported? So where are you?"

"Mexico, pendejo! Listen, you remember that cash I asked you to stash for me?"

"Fuuuuuck...yeah."

"Well I need it. Get your ass down here to Juarez."

"Juarez? That's a long way from San Diego!"

"Yeah, no shit. Just get here. I need money."

"Damn, well about that money-"

"What?"

"Well, I might have borrowed some."

Juan took a deep breath and then let it out. "How much is left?"

"Ten Gs."

"Fuck. You spent five thousand of my money?"

"Are you gonna kill me now? I mean, I thought you were gonna be gone a long time, so I figured I´d have time to pay you back. I promise!"

"I´m not gonna kill you. Just be here tomorrow. And bring the ten Gs."

"Palabra?" Crazy asked, meaning that if Juan gave his word as a man.

"Palabra. Now get the fuck to driving, mother fucker! I will be waiting on the main drag in front of a place called Tito's." Juan hung up. He walked over to the man who rented the phones.

"I got no money until tomorrow."

The man´s face contorted, as if Juan had just stabbed him. He looked carefully at Juan, studying him, looking for something of value. Juan had no jewelry, no watch, nothing. The man shook his head, clearly disappointed. He waved his hand for Juan to go. Juan didn't know why the guy didn't just call the police, but he was grateful that he didn't. That would have been a rough start to his new found freedom.

Juan walked out of the telephone rental place and stood on the street, absorbing every detail. He saw some gangster types on a corner, laughing, but he could tell that they had their guard up. It was obvious they were taking care of something, probably drugs or guns, or both.

A woman who was clearly high on drugs approached him. She held out some lollipops, waving them in front of his face. She was cute, but Juan saw the needle marks in her arms, legs, and her neck. *She is pretty fucked up if she had blown out all her veins and had to shoot up into her neck,* Juan thought.

"Five pesos."

"Got no money, babe. Just got deported."

She smiled. "Sorry to hear that, handsome. Here you go," she said, handing him a lollipop. "You can pay me later."

He smiled back. "I will. You can count on that. Palabra."

Juan sat down on the street curb, his stomach rumbling. The sun was beginning to set. It would be a long night.

Chapter Twelve

Juan spent the night exploring downtown Juarez. He walked up a side street and was accosted by tall transsexuals. They were all tall with thick legs and ridiculously round asses. As he passed by, each one would grab his crotch. Although he was horny, he ignored them, telling them he had no money. One girl-boy offered him services for free. He almost accepted, but he kept walking. *I didn't get out of the pinta just to hook up with more ass-pussy*, he thought.

Juan walked into a strip club where a pretty young girl was dancing away to the tune of a reggeton song. He went straight to the bathroom, and as he entered, he noticed a chubby waiter with a thick mustache almost following him in. When he walked out, the waiter was there, ready to take his order. There were only two customers in the place. The girl he had seen when he had entered was no longer dancing, and he decided to make that his excuse to leave.

"No girls dancing? What kind of a strip club is this?"

The waiter's face changed, angry that there was no one dancing. "Boss, they are just changing girls. There will be another one in just a minute."

"I like strip clubs that are professional. There should always be a girl ready to dance. Later." The waiter stood at the doorway, watching him leave, like a forlorn dog that watches as his master leaves the home.

Juan walked over to the main drag of Juarez, his stomach reminding him of his lack of attention to it as he passed by a half of block full of small restaurants. He ignored it and his thirst, and he sat back down next to Tito's, one of the first bars on the busy strip. When the bar closed and the loud music ended, he drifted in and out of sleep.

Suddenly, two cops awakened him, one of them giving him a nudge with his booted foot. Juan sprung to his feet, and the two officers stepped back startled. One had his hand on his gun, still holstered. Juan assumed the familiar position against the wall, hands and legs spread out. It was second nature to him.

"Look, Rodriguez, we didn't even have to tell him to do anything." The bigger of the two cops said, as he began to search Juan. "So, where is your identification?"

"Don't have one. Just got deported."

The cop laughed. "Are you even Mexican? You have a terrible accent." The cop finished patting Juan down and motioned for him to turn around. Juan did, keeping his hands visible to the cops.

"Yeah, I'm Mexican, just been in the U.S. for a long time."

"There's a shelter a few blocks from here. Why don't you go there, get something to eat and drink, *paisano*."

"Thanks, officers. I got a friend on his way. Should be here any minute."

"Fine. Just stay out of trouble. We don't need any more trouble in Juarez."

"No, sir. I'll be good." He made his hands into the sign of prayer and bowed his head down. The cops laughed and departed.

Crazy showed up around six in the morning. Juan was tired of sitting on the cold curb of the street, and he quickly got into Crazy's Yukon which was complete with numerous aftermarket additions. After clasping hands and half-hugging, Crazy handed Juan the cash and a .40 cal pistol. Juan smiled as he felt the weight of the loaded gun in his hand. Crazy looked uncomfortable, as if he had just handed Death his scythe.

"Don't worry, Crazy. I ain't gonna kill you. How would you pay me the money you owe me then?"

Crazy laughed, nervously. Juan didn't smile or laugh. Crazy quit laughing.

"I'll be in touch. You just be ready to do business."

Crazy left. Juan really did not want him around anyhow. He had plans, and they didn't include another man. He walked down the busy strip until he saw the man that previously told him that he could get him anything he wanted.

"Remember me?"

"Yeah, chief. What you need?"

"A girl. Young. Pretty. *Tight*."

"Just follow me. I know a place that's got a bunch of girls, like fifteen, sixteen years old."

"That'll work."

The man led Juan about eight blocks to an old, green hotel. Three girls, two really skinny, stood outside. As Juan and the man approached, the girls converged upon the men, each trying to get Juan to pick one.

"How much?"

"Twenty dollars, room included."

"No, how much for the three?"

The least skinny girl paused for a moment. "Sixty."

"I'll give you a hundred and twenty, and I want all three of you for an hour."

"I'll have to ask the boss. Wait a minute."

The girl entered the hotel, and Juan could see through the screen that she was talking to a man behind the front desk. She nodded and returned outside.

"One hundred and fifty."

"Deal."

Juan walked into the hotel with the three girls and up the stairs to an almost clean room. The last girl in turned and shut the door behind them.

Chapter Thirteen

Juan paid the man at the front desk twenty dollars so that he could sleep in the room in which he had just had an orgy, and he was given a key. He needed a key if he wanted to lock the door. The door had been open when he arrived with the girls, but he understood. He went back upstairs to the room and closed and locked the door. Several used condoms were on the floor, but they were his, so he didn't worry about it. He just lay on the bed, his hands behind his head. He was thinking about money when he fell asleep.

"Hey mother fucker, spread that ass open. You are too tight. I don't fit."

Juan grimaced in pain as the bigger man tried to penetrate him. Slowly, he closed his hand around the shank that he had hidden behind the bed post.

"Spooky, just let me turn around, and I'll put my legs up around my head so you can get in easier."

Spooky smiled, obviously pleased with the idea. "Yeah, bitch, now you're comin' around."

Juan turned around and thrust the shank deeply into Spooky's throat, over and over again. Spooky fell on top of him, blood shooting out of the holes made by the shank. Juan struggled to remove him, but the man's dead weight was too much for Juan's strength. He struggled more and wanted to scream.

Then he woke up, once again in his motel room, in Juarez. Dripping with sweat, he got up to take a shower. He turned on what he figured to be the hot water, let it run, and disrobed. He checked the water, but it was still cold. Frustrated, he shut the knob off and tried the other one, once again letting the water run. When the water from the other side didn't get warm either, Juan realized that there was no hot water and jumped into the cold shower. *Even the damn pinta had warm water*, he thought.

After searching for soap to no avail, Juan rinsed himself as best as he could, watching the water run over the many tattoos he had on his chest, arms, and stomach. He shut off the water and dried himself with a towel that was probably older than he was. He looked at himself in the mirror and turned halfway to admire his favorite tattoo. A beautiful drawn Virgen de Guadalupe in black prison ink stared back at him. It had taken a year to ink. The artist, a skinny guy named Triste, was dead now, and the Virgin was his last work. Juan had told him that no one else could have this tattoo. He had to understand that this Virgin had to be very special, and that when another inmate asked for one similar, no matter on what part of the body, he would have to decline.

Juan had been the leader of the cell block, controlling almost all of the Mexicans in the prison. He even had power outside of the prison, running a large gang in East Los Angeles. A leader of the Mexican mafia, a veterano, or veteran, as they called the old time gangsters, moved in and seized power. He had ordered Triste to ink the same tattoo on him and then torch Juan. However, Juan was a step ahead and had men very loyal to him acting as double agents, supposedly working for the veterano as his personal bodyguards. Juan walked right into the cell while Triste worked on him, doused them with a mixture he smuggled from the metal shop, and lit them both on fire.

Juan knew why he had been the leader. It wasn't because of his natural leadership skills; he didn't have any that he knew of. It wasn't because he was kind and fair; he wasn't. In fact, he was a cold-hearted killer with incredible instincts and a flare for cruelty. That was why he was the leader. His loyalist men acted out of fear and because Juan had done something for them. Everyone in prison who was anyone had at least one enemy. Juan ensured that anyone that worked for him didn't have enemies. Anyone that disrespected him or his people was executed. Anyone that betrayed them, looked at them the wrong way, or talked behind their backs was killed. But now he was out of jail, and for the first time since he was very young, Juan felt alone.

Juan pulled the .40 cal from under his pillow and shoved it into the front of his shorts. The long t-shirt he wore concealed it well. He went down the stairs and threw the room key at the man behind the front desk and walked out. As he departed, he noticed a man standing against the wall of the hotel. The man pretended not to notice Juan. Another man was on the opposite side of the street, also pretending not to see him. Juan knew they both saw him, and if they were both acting as if they didn't see him, it was because they were there for bad reasons. He hadn't been in Juarez long enough to have any enemies. Juan guessed that one of the girls must have revealed to someone about a man with significant money, or maybe it was even the man at the front desk. Regardless of the reason, Juan was fairly sure that they were there to rob him. He walked very quickly and turned the corner of the street. It was dark now, probably around nine at night. He pulled out his pistol and kept it at his waist and tight to his body, waiting for the men to come around the corner.

When the first man turned the corner, he only saw the barrel of the .40 as Juan placed the tip directly against his forehead. Juan pulled the trigger, and the pistol boomed, the bullet entering the skull and exiting through the back of his head. The man fell to his knees, then onto his back like some kind of a contortionist. The other man, hearing the shot, stopped short of the corner and turned around to run. But Juan was upon him and shot him several times in the back. The man fell face forward, landing hard without using his hands to break the fall. Juan stood over him and placed one last bullet into the back of the man's head. He looked around for witnesses, but the people in Juarez were used to this kind of thing. No one was around or showed their faces if there were. A red Ford king cab pickup was slowly driving down the road. Juan didn't know if they had seen him or not either, but he decided that he had already done enough damage and began to walk quickly in the other direction.

Hearing sirens, Juan walked into a night club. A waiter was eager to take his order, and Juan asked for a beer, Tecate. He sat down at a table facing the door with his back to the wall. The waiter brought him the Tecate, and as Juan pulled out a hundred dollar bill, the waiter's eyes widened. Juan thought that it would have been smart to have gotten some change before paying for the hookers, the hotel, and now this drink. It would have probably saved him some trouble. The waiter took the bill.

"One hundred dollars, sir."

"That's right. Bring my change back correctly, or I'll break you."

"Ye-yes sir, of course."

Juan stared at the entrance, waiting for cops to enter at any moment, but they didn't. Instead, a cowboy with many gold chains and rings arrived along with another man. The second man was taller with boots as well, but overall, he was less well dressed and wore a cap instead of a cowboy hat. The cowboy looked at Juan, pointed, and the men walked towards him. Juan removed the pistol from his shorts and kept it under the table with his focus on the better dressed of the two men. The cowboy put his hands up in front of him in a non-menacing manner.

"Hey, we're not here to fight with you, killer. Just the opposite. We want to offer you a job."

Juan still held the pistol in his lap, ready to fire at first sign of trouble. The cowboy slid one of the metal chairs out to sit down and looked at Juan, as if asking permission. Juan nodded in consent, and he sat down. The other man was still standing, and his hand firmly held the grip of a pistol he had tucked in the front of his pants. But he wasn't really watching Juan; instead he was watching the entrance, as if suspecting someone to rush in behind them. Juan noticed that he had some tattoos on his neck.

"I'm Juanito, but everyone calls me Johnny." He stuck out his hand. Juan shook it, the way gangsters do, and the cowboy followed suit.

"I'm Juan. I don't know what everyone calls me. Probably *hijo de puta*."

The cowboy laughed, retracting his hand. "Tocayo." He said, meaning that they have the same name. "You new here?"

"Yeah. Just got deported."

Johnny shook his head. "Fucking United States. They can't get enough of us to do their dirty work, pick their fields, sell them dope." he said, smiling, "But they can't wait to get rid of us, either."

"I really don't blame them for wanting to get rid of me."

Johnny nodded, understanding. "Well, Tocayo, let me tell you something. I got an eye for talent. I saw you take care of a situation just a little bit ago, and I told El Turco," he pointed at the other man, eyes still fixed on the entrance, hand on the pistol grip, "I said, this is a man with talent. Your kind of talent can be a great asset in my organization. I work with a group of people that are also new to Juarez. I am from Sinaloa myself, and Turco is from Tijuana. We are having some territorial issues with the other organization here. They said that they were here first and don't need to share. We don't plan to leave, though. I think you get what I mean."

Juan did and nodded. This Johnny was very charismatic, and when he smiled, Juan almost smiled right along with him. Almost.

"Okay, let us say I am interested in this job offer. What do I have to do, get initiated or something?"

"No. Nothing like that. This isn't a gang; it's a business. I would give you a task, you would carry it out, and I would pay you well for it. That's it. Of course, you wouldn't be allowed to work for anyone else. We are called the Gente Nueva, and we are a very jealous business."

"Of course. Let me think about it."

"Sure. Take your time. How do I get a hold of you?"

"Shit. I don't have a phone or cell."

The man removed a cell phone from his pocket. He had a Blackberry in a case hooked to his belt. "Take this. I´ll be in touch."

Chapter Fourteen

The Army captain was murdered at seven-thirty in the evening. The next day, at three in the morning, Felipe and his accomplices left the safe house. Felipe drove his cousin Jorge to his house and then continued to a motel, where he rented a room and parked his car in the attached garage. After entering the room, Felipe closed the garage door and sat on the edge of the bed. The television was on, and a woman was groaning in faked ecstasy on the screen. He watched the porno and lit a cigarette. After a few minutes, he picked up the motel room phone and dialed zero.

"Reception."

"Bring me a hot girl."

"Okay, I'll send them over. It will be about twenty minutes, though, because I have to call them. They don't stay here."

"Fine." Felipe hung up the phone.

After about forty minutes, Felipe heard a car arrive outside. He looked out the window and saw that the girls arrived in a Chevrolet Geo Metro. There were four girls, one in the front passenger seat and three in the back seat. The driver was an older man with graying hair, and he exited the vehicle and knocked on the garage door. Felipe opened the garage door, and the man called for the girls. They all got out of the car, giggling and whispering among each other, and they lined up for Felipe.

"How much?"

"Fifty dollars for an hour."

Felipe looked at the girls, studying each one. They all smiled at him, except for a pretty, short girl with long black hair. She turned her head away, seemingly shy. Felipe pointed to her.

"That one." He pulled out a hundred dollar bill. "Here's two hours."

The man took the money and put it in his pocket. The other girls shrugged, returned to the car with the driver, and they departed. As the shy girl entered the room, Felipe closed the garage door. He walked into the room and shut the door, locking it behind him. The girl sat on the edge of the bed, staring at the porno.

"How old are you?"

The girl looked at him, then away. "Nineteen."

"You look sixteen."

"I'm nineteen."

"Okay. Why are you still dressed?"

She laughed as she slipped off her clothes; Felipe did as well. Her eyes grew wide when she saw the size of Felipe's penis. Felipe smiled, shut off the television and took her, roughly.

Afterward, Felipe lit a cigarette. The girl smiled, her eyes closed. Felipe didn't know why, but he didn't want her to leave, as he normally did. He turned on the television and changed the channel to an old black and white Pedro Infante movie. The girl stood, and her perfect, naked body was illuminated by the television's light. She walked to the bathroom, and Felipe heard her urinate. Then he heard her turn on the shower.

He took a drag of his cigarette and let the smoke out. He doubted that she had been working professionally for very long, but she had been incredibly good in bed. He decided he would ask her when she got out of the shower. After a while, Felipe heard her turn off the water. She appeared wrapped in a motel towel, her brown skin looking even darker against the white towel.

"Where are you from?"

"Veracruz. And you?"

"Chihuahua." Felipe replied. "Been in Juarez long?"

"Two months. Came to work at a factory to help my parents in Veracruz, but it closed down a few weeks ago." She looked away. "So I got this job."

Felipe liked this girl, unlike the regular whores he hired. She was different somehow. She reminded him of his mother.

"Can I have your number? Your personal number?"

Ruby gave it to him.

Chapter Fifteen

Felipe picked up the stacks of twenties on the Silva's Silva's desk and shoved them into his pockets without counting the money. Silva was still on the phone, as he had been since Felipe had arrived. Silva waved for him to leave, and Felipe happily obliged. He hated this condescending bastard that didn't even have the decency to get off the phone while he did business with him. It was a serious lack of respect, and Felipe vowed silently to himself that one day he would pull the lawyer's tongue out from his throat just as the Colombians did. He slammed the office door behind him, scaring the lawyer's attractive secretary. She attempted to remain unaffected by the chaos.

Felipe returned to his truck where Jorge was waiting for him and removed the money from his pockets. He counted Jorge's share and handed it to him. Next, he counted money for Mr. Fresa and Sad Face, set the money packs aside, and pocketed the rest. He started the truck and backed it out, peeling the tires as he did. Jorge laughed as a young boy does when his father does something silly.

Felipe and Jorge drove to one of the two Starbucks in Juarez where Mr. Fresa was waiting with an attractive young woman. They waited in the truck for Mr. Fresa. When he saw Felipe and Jorge, Mr. Fresa said something to the girl, gave her a kiss, and then he came outside. Jorge got out of the truck to let in Mr. Fresa, who scooted over to the middle as Juan then returned to the passenger seat. Felipe handed Mr. Fresa his share of money for the job, and Mr. Fresa, without counting the money, placed the bills in his pockets. After shaking hands with Felipe, Mr. Fresa exited the vehicle and returned to Starbucks. Then Felipe and Jorge screeched off again.

As Felipe pulled up to a stop light, he honked his truck's horn. A man dressed like a gangster but with his face painted like a clown came running and jumped in the bed of the pickup. Felipe drove to the parking lot of a store that had gone out of business, and Jorge got out letting Sad Face in the cab of the truck. Jorge motioned for the clown-gangster to move over, and he got back in the truck after Sad Face had scooted to the middle. Felipe gave the clown his money, and they shook hands. Once again, Jorge got out of the truck, the clown exited, and they drove away. In his rear view mirror, Felipe saw Sad Face counting his money.

Now that the money was distributed, Felipe and Jorge decided to go eat carnitas. They drove about fifteen minutes until they reached the edge of the city, where they stopped at a restaurant that only served fried pig meat and chicharrones. A skinny, poorly dressed man whistled and supposedly helped them to park. Felipe and Jorge got out and locked the truck.

"Don't worry, boss. I'll take good care of the truck. You want me to clean it?"

Felipe turned around and looked at the man. "Fine."

Felipe turned back around, and they entered the restaurant which smelled of burning hickory and pork. A waitress, who was nothing much to look at, walked casually over to Felipe and Jorge and told them that they could sit wherever they wished, as she handed them menus. The men walked over to the farthest corner from the entrance and sat, Felipe with his back to the wall. The waitress, in long shorts and a t-shirt, asked them what they wanted, and they ordered beers, carnitas, and chicharrones.

A few minutes later the waitress brought the beers. Felipe and Jorge quickly drank the Tecates and signaled to the waitress to bring more, which she did.

"Would you like the bucket of ten beers, better?" she asked, obviously not wanting to have to keep walking to their table.

"Sure. " Felipe said.

The waitress left, and after about ten minutes, she returned with a metal pail filled with ice and ten bottles of beer. She left again, returning later with the pork and a green Chile sauce that smelled delicious, but it was probably incredibly spicy.

Felipe and Jorge drank beer, ate pork, and laughed at old war stories, similar to Mexico's favorite assassination bloopers which included men that screamed like girls, or begged for their lives, or had even offered their sisters' bodies in return for mercy. As they exchanged many stories, the hours passed and three more buckets of beer passed as well. Slightly inebriated, Felipe paid the bill, and the men departed the restaurant. Jorge handed ten dollars to the parking attendant who thanked them excessively.

After leaving the restaurant, Felipe and Jorge drove until they saw a convenience store where they stopped to buy more beer. Jorge returned from the store with a smile, carrying two bags full of ice and beer. The two men drank and cruised and talked about the old days in their home town, Mapimi, Durango. When the beer ran out, they bought more.

After ten o'clock, the stores cannot legally sell alcohol, so Felipe and Jorge went to a clandestine store and purchased more beer. These stores were often small grocery stores with a little bit of everything and were usually run by the family in part of the owner's house. The stores would stock up on beer and liquor and sell it illegally at an elevated cost after ten o'clock.

When Felipe saw that Jorge was passing out because of his drunkenness, he drove Jorge to his house. He helped Jorge out of the truck, half carrying, half dragging him to the front door, where his extremely angry wife was waiting for him. She didn't like Felipe, and Felipe didn't care for her, but they both cared for Jorge, so they tolerated each other.

Felipe left Jorge's house and called Ruby, the girl from the motel. She had given him her cell number.

Chapter Sixteen

"I'm working," Ruby answered, in a hushed voice.

"Quit. I want you to move in with me."

"I can't. You probably don't even have a house."

"Quit. I'll give you the money to rent one. Meet me at the same motel in an hour."

"Are you serious or just drunk, Felipe?"

"Serious. Very serious. Have I told you to quit yet?" She laughed. "See you at the motel."

"Okay," she whispered.

Felipe arrived at the motel and got a room. He then called Ruby to give her the room number. She was there in less than an hour along with her pimp. Felipe felt his blood rising. He opened the garage door with his pistol in hand and walked out to the car to meet them.

"I thought I told you to quit."

"I tried Felipe, but Mario says that you have to pay him for the night at least."

"Bullshit." He put his gun to Mario's head. Mario whimpered and trembled.

"Shut the fuck up, Mario. Get the hell out of here, don't come back, and don't bother Ruby either or I will kill you and anyone you are with. I mean anyone. That means your kids, your wife, your mother. *Anyone.*"

Mario, still sitting in the car, nodded. Felipe let him drive away, and Ruby and he went into the room, Felipe closing the garage behind them.

"Did you mean that?"

Felipe frowned, not liking being questioned. "Mean what?"

"That you'd kill whoever he was with."

"Maybe." Felipe paused and thought for a moment. "Yes."

For security, Felipe and Ruby left and drove to a different motel where they rented a room. Felipe was too drunk to have sex with Ruby, so they watched television until he fell asleep. Felipe liked sleeping when he was drunk, because he didn't have nightmares. When he awoke in the morning, Ruby was already dressed.

"I'm ready to rent a house. And I need to send money to my parents."

Felipe blinked, the words taking a moment to penetrate his sleepy mind. "Fine."

Felipe retrieved a newspaper sent from the front desk. As they ate breakfast, Felipe and Ruby circled classifieds for rental properties. After selecting the best five properties, Felipe called and scheduled appointments to see three of the five properties. Felipe never liked to remain in one place because that made him an easier target. But something had happened to him when he met Ruby, and he wanted to be with her.

Following breakfast, Felipe and Ruby departed the motel to look at the rental properties. After seeing several houses, Ruby decided on the third property.

"It is perfect," she said.

After renting the furnished house, Felipe gave money to Ruby to send to her parents. He wanted to impress her, so he sent them sent a thousand dollars. Ruby was impressed, and they immediately went back to their new rented home and had sex on a bed without sheets.

Afterwards, Ruby told Felipe that she needed to buy items for the house as well as clothes. She had left all her clothes at the pimp's house where she and the other girls stayed. Tired and somewhat hung over, Felipe gave her money and told her to get a cab and do all the shopping that she needed to complete. Genuinely grateful, she smiled and gave him a big kiss.

Felipe fell asleep on the sheet-less, pillow-less bed. It didn't take long before he was deep in another nightmare. He was running from somebody or some bodies, he didn't know whom, and his legs seemed as if they were made of lead. Then he felt cold hands with steely grips upon him, and they dragged him down to the ground. He shut his eyes tightly, but he could still see the skeletal figures that were upon him. One figure began digging with his hands as fast as he could, with superhuman strength and speed. When the hole was very deep, the figures dragged Felipe and threw him in the hole. Then they all threw dirt over him, burying him alive. Felipe woke up, his face in the pillow, gasping.

Ruby arrived several hours later with dishes, sheets, bedspreads, pillows, a small television, clothes, shoes, and food. After she was finished arranging the new household items, she retrieved a box and handed it to Felipe. The box was covered in Christmas wrapping, even though it was July.

Felipe, surprised, asked, "For me?"

"Of course!" Felipe opened the box and revealed a pair of expensive black crocodile boots. He was speechless; no one had ever given him anything.

Chapter Seventeen

Saul smiled, a big, wide grin, full of love and tenderness. It was an expressive, open smile that was not at all what would be expected from a crime reporter, much less a crime reporter in one of the most violent cities in North America. His wife returned the smile. Edilia, still a very beautiful woman at the age of forty, was very much in love with Saul as he was with her. She constantly worried about his safety, but she knew that he would not be happy doing anything else in his life. He loved reporting, he loved *The Juarez Daily*, and he loved Juarez. He loved his city and expected nothing in return.

"So, now are you really going to tell me what happened tonight, or are you still going to avoid the issue?"

Saul's answer was a snore, long and loud. Edilia knew now that he was working on something very dangerous, so dangerous that he was not about to let her in on any details. She also knew that there was no way she could dissuade him from continuing to work on the story, whatever it was.

"Please, Saul, just be careful. We need you."

When Edilia awoke, Saul had already been up, working diligently on his laptop. He saw her stretching and smiled. He was always smiling.

"God, what time is it Saul?" Edilia asked, her voice hoarse with sleepiness.

"Early."

"How early?"

"Five."

"Oh God. Saul, you are crazy."

Edilia rolled over and fell back asleep. Her dreams were troubled; a series of thunderstorms were passing over the horizon, raining blood. Saul was riding backwards on a horse, and his usually constant smile was turned viciously upside down. Edilia and their daughters, dressed in their finest clothes, were at a wedding. The dreams made no sense to her, but she felt terror.

When she awoke, she felt tired and anxious. She smelled eggs and chorizo. Poor Saul, she thought, made breakfast already because his lazy wife did not wake up in time. She climbed out of the bed, put on the robe she had hanging on a chair, and walked downstairs to the kitchen. The smell of the eggs and chorizo made her hungry, and her stomach growled, loudly. Saul was wearing her flowery apron.

"You look silly."

"Thanks. Good morning to you, too. Do you want your eggs in a burrito?"

"Sure. Let me get the girls up."

"Already did. They already ate."

"Wow! How efficient you are. Want my job, too?"

"No way! I couldn't handle it. Better stick to something easy, like crime reporting. Housewifery should be left to the professionals."

Saul drove his white 1993 Toyota Camry to the large *Juarez Daily* building, weaving in and out of the lanes while avoiding the buses and ridiculously slow traffic. He also attempted to stay out of the way of those who tried their best to hit maximized speed between the stoplights. When one of the many speeders honked, Saul smiled and kindly got out of his way. If the guy who had honked at him just happened to be one of Juarez's many killers, with an AK-47 at his side, Saul didn't want to be the one to anger him. He pulled into the employee parking area at the back of the office building, and after he removed the key from the ignition, he grabbed the club and placed it on the steering wheel, locking it tight. A guard attended the parking area, but it was force of habit to always exercise caution and safety. Saul exited the car, locking the car before he closed the door. He walked briskly to the rear entrance.

As Saul walked the hallway consisting of large glass walls, coworkers smiled and waved at him. Everyone at the office seemed to like Saul. It was hard not to like him; he nearly always wore a contagious smile, was upbeat, and never complained unless he was talking about the Mexican government and their lack of responsibility to its people.

He walked into his small office with a messy desk, shoved some papers aside in order to put down his outdated laptop, and connected it to the power source. If he didn't connect the laptop immediately, it would shut down after about a minute. He reread the stories he had written the previous day concerning executions in three different locations all within a one hour period. He decided to condense the three stories and titled it, "Three Executions in One Hour Period." After printing the article, he exited his office and walked down the glass corridor to deliver his work to the editor. Michelle greeted him warmly, rising and giving him a hug when he entered.

"Well, there you have it. Friday evening's newest murders."

"Great. When is this going to end?" Michelle asked, rhetorically.

He shrugged, knowing that she expected no answer. Michelle's hair was cut short, almost cropped. She was average height and weight, attractive, without calling too much attention to herself. She wore black slacks that accentuated her curves and a white blouse that highlighted her full chest. People in the office often commented that they thought she was a lesbian, but Saul didn't believe that it was true, nor would he have cared should it have been so. Saul respected her greatly because it was very difficult for a woman to arrive at a position of power in Mexico and even harder in the state of Chihuahua. She was also very good at her job.

"Well, at least we have plenty of news to report."

She smiled. "I suppose."

Saul´s cell phone rang, shattering the silence that had momentarily overtaken the room. He excused himself with a motion of his hand, and Michelle nodded understandingly.

"Saavedra."

The voice on the other end spoke in a hushed and hurried tone. "Saul, get to 413 N. Panama, right away."

"Understood. Thanks."

"My police contact."

"Did he say what it was?"

"No, but it must be bad. He sounded nervous, and he isn't the nervous type."

"Well, go get it. And be careful."

"Thanks Michelle. See you."

"Yeah, later."

Saul walked quickly out of the editor´s office, shutting her door behind him, and he locked up his office as he passed by. His notebook and camera were already in the car. Half-running through the parking lot, he got in his car, turned the key in the ignition, and drove away. The parking guard barely returned his wave as he departed. Saul didn't know very many friendly guards in Juarez.

Saul didn't blame them, for they were exposed to dangerous positions without any real weapons. Also, they were responsible for many employees and their possessions, and their pay was not compensatory. Combined, this would lead anyone to be unfriendly.

Saul parked about a block from the address given to him by his police contact. He usually paid his contact a small stipend for any important information leading to a halfway decent story. There was no greater motivator than money. It moved anything and everything in Mexico.

As Saul was getting out of his car, he hung his journalist identification around his neck. Officer Vazquez met Saul at the yellow tape barrier that cordoned the crime scene. Soldiers and federal police armed with large caliber automatic weapons roamed the scene, trampling any possible clues and evidence that may have existed. So-called forensic specialists were taking pictures of the body and the scene. A man, a woman, and a child were slouched over in a car, blood all over their bodies and the inside of the car. Shattered glass was lying around the bullet-ridden vehicle.

"Awful, isn't it?" said Officer Vasquez. "The man is an ex-city police officer, and the other two are his wife and daughter. I knew the guy. He quit about two years ago after he had some trouble with the new chief of police. He's been dealing coke ever since."

"Vazquez, this is the worst yet. Homicide has more than tripled since last year, but children? This is too much, even for the mafia."

"Things have changed with these fucking hit men the mafia is using nowadays. There's no honor, no limits. They are always trying to make the executions more horrific so that they can scare the rival. They don't just go after the mobster, but his entire family. Saul, something has to be done."

Saul snapped some pictures of the scene. The forensic team was either having a smoke break or they were finished. He zoomed in on the car, focused the lens, and released the camera's shutter. The child, who appeared to be all of four years old, was still clutching her stuffed bear. Saul reasoned that maybe she had thought that the bear would protect her from the man or men that shot her family. Tears ran down Saul's cheeks as he finished photographing the scene, his daughters' faces in his mind' eye. He struggled to steady his hands as he took the pictures.

When he finished, he returned to his car and vomited just outside the driver's door. The time following the horrific scene he had covered passed by slowly, almost dreamlike. Actually, the time was nightmare-like, and at some point, the work day finally ended, and Saul returned home.

"Earth to Saul, are you there?" Edilia asked as she set the table.

"Sorry babe. What did you ask me?"

"Nothing. Ximena did."

Saul turned to see his nine-year old daughter staring at him, obviously waiting for an answer. He gave her a tight hug, and Maria ran to him as well, her five year old arms wrapping around his neck.

"Sorry Mija. Didn't hear what you said."

"Daddy, can we go to the park after dinner?"

"It is cold outside."

Ximena looked at him with sad, pleading eyes. "Fine. Sure, I'll take you."

The time spent at dinner and the park was a blur for Saul. He felt as if he were a zombie, half dead to the world. They visited the park that was a few blocks away from their house, a small area with little grass, a few trees, and some standard swings, slides, and see-saws. It was not his favorite park by far, but Saul was of little humor to go anywhere else. He sat and watched the girls play instead of playing with them as he usually would. The temperature was about fifty degrees, so they all wore their jackets, but there was no wind, so the evening was pleasant.

They went back home before nine and put the girls to bed. As he lay in bed, Edilia was in the bathroom washing her face and brushing her teeth. Saul's mind returned again to the crime scene he had witnessed earlier. He had seen multiple dead bodies over the years, but never an entire family. He had seen the dead bodies of fifteen and sixteen year old girls, reported on the many deaths of women in Juarez, but he had never seen something like what he witnessed today. The scene meant much more than just a dead trafficker; it meant a total disregard for what are the most sacred things in Mexican society - the mother and children. It was the beginning of a new generation of killers, heartless and without any honor or limitations.

Edilia closed the bathroom door behind her as she entered the bedroom. "Saul, what's going on?"

"Oh God, Edilia, I don't even know where to begin."

"Look, if you don't feel like talking about it, I understand." She sat down on the bed next to him, caressing his face. "But if it makes you feel better, then just start at the beginning, and don't worry how bad it is; I can handle it."

Saul took a deep breath and told Edilia all about the scene to include his trembling and vomiting after seeing his girls' faces when he took the pictures. Tears trickled out of the corners of her eyes, and they both cried as they hugged each other. He slept badly as his dreams were once again filled with random violence and dead people. In the morning, he could barely open his eyes when it was time to get up, and Edilia motivated him with a delicious breakfast. Later in the afternoon, Saul went to the office and remained there until he left to cover a house fire. He really had no desire to be out in the streets, but that was part of the job requirement.

The house fire turned out to be a minor blaze, which the firemen extinguished quickly, and no one had been injured. It was late, after ten at night. On his way home, Saul swerved the car to avoid the body of a man in the street, covered by a black trash bag. His heart began to pound. He hit the brakes and eased the vehicle to the side of the road. Saul exited his car, closing the door behind him, and walked towards to the seemingly lifeless body. Orange cowboy boots stuck out from under the black garbage bag, the body's feet pointing toward the sidewalk. Saul discovered that the body wasn't actually in the bag, but that the bag was spread over the body as if it were a blanket. As Saul looked closer, he noticed the body was breathing.

Saul hesitantly uncovered the man and found that he was not dead, dying, or even injured, just drunk. Saul laughed, partly at himself and partly out of relief. He attempted to wake the drunkard, but the man only mumbled as drool ran out of the side of his mouth. Saul dragged him to the sidewalk and called 066 on his cell phone, the emergency number. The phone rang and rang, but no one answered. At that moment, he saw a patrol car coming down the road, so he hung up the cell phone and waved down the car for assistance. The cops pulled to the side in front of Saul, and the driver rolled down his window. He stared at Saul without speaking.

"I called the emergency number, but no one answered. Could you call an ambulance?"

"He's not dead?" the cop asked in a matter-of-fact manner.

"No! He is extremely drunk, might even have alcohol poisoning. And as cold as it is, he'll be dead before morning."

"We'll handle it. Best be on your way; it is dangerous out here." The driver looked at the other cop and smirked as he spoke. The cops drove away.

Saul returned to his car and waited for assistance to arrive. After fifteen minutes passed, he realized that they had no intention of doing anything to help the drunken man. Saul again got out of his vehicle and opened the rear driver's side door of his car. He then walked over to the inebriated man, grabbed him under both shoulders, and dragged him to the car. The man reeked of sweat and booze, and Saul gagged. Edilia surely would not have approved of this, he thought. Saul pulled, pushed, and otherwise struggled to get the man into the back seat and to shut the door, pushing the man farther in with it, much as one does when closing an over-stuffed suitcase.

Saul drove to a small clinic in downtown Juarez. He checked on the man before exiting the vehicle. *Good, still breathing.* He quickly got out of the car and headed toward the clinic's front entrance and rang the doorbell. An annoying buzz could be heard on the other side of the wall. A few minutes later, an older woman, thin with gray hair, appeared at the door and opened a small sliding window on the top half of the door. She stared at Saul, not saying a word.

"Good evening."

She still stared. Saul waited for her response, but her silence continued.

"I found this man on the street, extremely drunk, and he may have alcohol poisoning."

"Take him to the shelter or to the police." She shut the window and walked away briskly.

Saul stood agape at the entrance. *Edilia isn't going to be at all happy.* Saul returned to his car and drove home. When he entered his house, Saul explained to Edilia the situation he had just encountered.

"Have you completely lost your mind, Saul?"

"There is nowhere else to take him."

"He could be a killer, a drug addict, a felon for all you know!"

"I can't have his death on my conscience. It's forty-four degrees outside, and the guy is unconscious. I took him to a clinic, and they won't have him. The cops could care less. If you like, I will run around the rest of the night with him in the back of our car and possibly find a place that will take him."

Edilia frowned, shaking her head. "No. Put him in the garage. I'll bring you some old blankets and a bottle of water."

Saul smiled at her, hoping for a smile in return, but there was none. Edilia returned a few minutes later with the old blankets and a bottle of water. Saul pulled the man out of the car and did his best to lay him on top of a blanket, and he covered him up with another. The drunken man grunted and rolled on his side, a good sign that he was going to survive. Saul shut and locked the door leading to the garage, and Edilia lodged a chair underneath the doorknob for added security. She turned to look at Saul, placing her hands on her hips. Saul shrugged, and she hugged and kissed him.

"Glad you are okay, *Tonto*."

"You had me going there. Thought you were mad at me."

She pulled away from him. "Make no mistake, Saul, I'm not happy with the situation. But I love you just the way you are, no matter how foolish you may act."

"Oh. Thanks, I guess."

Edilia and Saul looked at each other and laughed. As they walked up the stairs, Saul followed Edilia with his hands on her butt.

Chapter Eighteen

Saul awoke early, well aware that a stranger was sleeping in the garage. He made coffee while Edilia got a few extra minutes of sleep, as it was Sunday. The smell of the coffee brewing must have awakened the stranger, and he knocked softly on the kitchen door that led to the garage. Saul braced himself and decided to open the door. The man's eyes were bloodshot and swollen, and he still reeked of alcohol.

"Good morning, sir. I seemed to have ended up in your garage last night."

"Yeah, you did. I picked you up from the middle of the street where you had been sleeping and brought you here."

"Where is *here*, exactly?"

Saul laughed. "You're still in Juarez. In the neighborhood called the Americas."

A look of relief appeared on the hung over man's face. "Good. I'm not too far away from my mother's place. My name is Angel."

He stuck out his open hand. Saul extended his hand and shook it gently.

"Angel, come on in. Let's have breakfast."

"I've been in enough trouble, already."

"Come on in. Have some coffee at least."

The man entered the kitchen. "Thanks, Saul."

Saul motioned for Angel to sit down at the kitchen table and he did. Saul set a cup of coffee on the table in front of Angel, as well as a jar with sugar, a spoon, and a can of condensed milk. Angel prepared his coffee.

"So tell me, Angel, what do you do for a living?"

"I'm a plumber."

"Noble profession. Glad you're not a *narco*."

"No. Never have even thought about being a drug dealer or anything like that. I might be a drunk, but my parents raised me right. I do all kinds of construction, too. Roofing, tile, stucco. You name it. Everything except electricity. Scares the hell out of me."

"Me too."

"So what do you do, Saul?"

"I write for the *Juarez Daily*."

"Wow. Good paper. My dad read it every day until he died last year. I still read it, sometimes. But I read the *PM* more."

Saul frowned as he sat down at the table and prepared his coffee. The men drank their coffee in silence, contemplating their perspective situations. Saul and Angel finished their coffee, and Saul picked up the two cups and placed them in the sink. Angel got up from the table and extended his hand again.

"Thanks for everything, Saul. Sorry about the *PM* thing." The men shook hands.

Saul laughed and shook his head. "Just wait a minute while I get my coat."

"Not necessary. I can walk. The cold will help get my head clear before I get to my mom's house."

"Sure. Well, take care young man."

"If you ever need some work done here, just let me know. You want my number?"

Saul grabbed his cell phone from the counter. "What is it?"

Angel dictated his number to Saul, and he entered it into his cell phone.

"And you better give me a deal!"

Angel smiled. "Definitely."

Angel left through the front door, and Saul watched him walk down the street after briefly getting his bearings. Saul shut the door and locked it. Edilia was just coming down the stairs, her hair in a bun and her eyes puffy.

"Was that our inebriated guest just leaving?"

"Yep."

"Well, that's a relief. I half expected to find you with a knife in your head or something."

"Nope. Hid the knives."

"So what's for breakfast?"

"Oh, so you expect me to cook today, too?"

"Yes."

"Well, get the girls ready. We'll have menudo."

"How come whenever I ask you to cook, Saul, we end up eating out?"

"Because I'm smart."

"Yes, you are indeed. A smart ass."

They laughed and got the girls up and ready. There was nothing like menudo and freshly baked, buttered bread on a cold winter morning.

Chapter Nineteen

"Two cops are parked by the bank on Zaragoza and Panamericana. The soldiers that are protecting them are inside the bank, and will be there for about ten more minutes," Johnny told Juan on his cell phone.

"I'll call you when those pigs have been made *chicharrones*."

Johnny laughed, a robust sound. "You do that. Better hurry."

Juan and his new partner, Tijuas, were only two minutes away. "Johnny says there are two cops in the parking lot by the bank."

"Fuck. What about the soldiers?" Soldiers had been accompanying the police ever since several cops had been killed while on duty. Juan was proud to say that he had killed three cops himself.

"The soldiers are inside the bank, so no worries. Get ready, we're almost there."

Tijuas checked to ensure his AK-47 was ready to fire. Juan parked his Ford Expedition behind the police truck, but left it running. The two men jumped out of the SUV, trained their weapons on the truck, and began firing. The cops, a woman and a man, never had a chance. The two men returned quickly to their SUV to escape.

As they drove away, Juan saw through his rear view mirror a soldier run out of the bank, conveniently too late to react to their aggression. He laughed as he took a joint out of an old mint box that he used to store rolled joints. He lit it, dragging deeply as he did. He held the smoke in and passed it to Tijuas.

"So why do they call you Tijuas?" He exhaled as he spoke.

"I'm from Tijuana," he said, pointing to the letters "TJ" tattooed on the side of his neck. He took a long puff from the joint and handed it back to Juan.

"Makes sense."

Juan removed the cell phone he had in his shirt pocket and called Johnny. "Done deal, two *chicharrones* have been served."

"Good job, *Tocayo*. You can pick up your paycheck at Queen's. There's a bonus in there for you, just don't tell Tijuas."

"Simon, boss."

Juan hung up and turned the SUV around, heading to downtown Juarez. Juan and Tijuas passed several vehicles with police and soldiers, but none seemed suspicious. Juan parked on the street in front of the strip club named Queen's. After scanning the area for suspicious people or police, Juan and Tijuas exited the vehicle after they were satisfied in the safety of their surroundings. The large metallic doors were heavy, and Juan pulled firmly on the right door. It opened slowly, and the two men entered the completely empty and dim bar. Tijuas sat at a nearby table while Juan went immediately to the bartender.

"Got something for me," Juan said directly, not asking.

The balding man with a thick mustache nodded as he reached for two envelopes from beneath the counter.

"For you," he said, handing Juan an envelope. "For him," he said, pointing to Tijuas and handing Juan the other envelope.

Juan didn't open his envelope, placing it immediately in his pocket. He walked to the table where Tijuas was sitting and handed him his envelope. After opening the seal, Tijuas counted the hundred dollar bills, smiling after he did. He slid the envelope into his back pocket as he stood. The men left the bar, carefully checking the area again for anyone suspicious.

"Hey Tijuas, want to get some tacos?"

"Hell yeah. Let's go somewhere expensive."

As the men drove, they became jammed behind slower traffic. Juan proceeded to pass a car, but Tijuas waved frantically to wait.

"No! Don't pass yet, Let's make a bet." The evil grin on Tijuas's face alerted Juan that he had something mischievous in mind.

"On what?"

"I bet that if we honk and get right on her ass that she will flip us off. And if she does, we kill her. And you pay me a thousand."

"And if she doesn't?"

"She lives, and I'll pay you a thousand."

"You're on."

Juan began honking incessantly, and he drove as close to her car as possible without colliding. The woman driver never even glanced, but she just continued staring straight ahead. As soon as she had an opportunity, the woman moved to the right lane to let them pass. Juan pulled the Ford Expedition in front of her car and forced her to stop on the shoulder of the road. Juan got out of his vehicle, walked over to her side of the car, and tapped on the window. The woman lowered the window, trembling as she did.

"Good thing you didn't flip us off. My buddy would have killed you." Juan removed five hundred dollars from his pocket and handed it to the woman.

"There's your share." She hesitated. "Don't worry, you earned it. See, we bet and I won. Take it."

Her hands shaking, the woman took the money. Juan returned to the SUV and drove away as both men laughed.

"I bet she shit her pants," Tijuas said.

Juan stopped the SUV right in the middle of the road. "How much for that bet?" Juan laughed and started driving again. Tijuas laughed too.

After a few minutes, Juan and Tijuas stopped at a small taco shop and bought four orders of pork tacos. The pork was on a vertically lined spic, a fire fueled by propane which cooked the meat as it slowly turned. The juices from a half pineapple dribbled down from above for flavor. Juan and Tijuas hastily ate the tacos.

"What do we do now?"

Juan thought for a moment. "We can get some bitches. Nothing like tuna after some good *carne asada*. Let's go to a massage parlor."

"Good idea."

There were ten different massage parlors in Juarez. There had been more in the past, but now that the *gringos* didn't cross the border anymore, a few had shut down. The massage parlor that Juan chose was on the second floor of a former apartment complex building. After walking up the stairs, the men knocked on the locked glass door.

Juan heard a lady yell, "Girls! Customers!" The darkly tinted glass door opened, and the men walked inside.

A heavy-set lady asked them, "Service or information?"

"Information."

"Forty dollars for an hour, a massage, and relations with the girl."

Juan smiled; there were a lot of perks to living in Mexico and having money, even more advantages than when he was living in the States. The lady led Juan to a room with a massage bed in the middle, and Tijuas to another similar room. After a parade of young, leggy women, Juan chose a girl with oriental eyes and hair as black as night that looked as if she were maybe seventeen. He was rough with her, but she was a good sport about it, so he tipped her well.

Relaxed and ready to party, the men left the parlor. They stopped at a drive-through liquor store and bought a twelve pack of Tecate. "Throw in some limes, chief," Juan told the man that was packing their beers. He did and also gave them some packets of salt. Juan tipped him five dollars, and as the men left the liquor store, Tijuas turned up the SUV's radio which was playing a song about a drug dealer that was killed in a blaze of gunfire.

Juan and Tijuas drove around downtown as they avoided checkpoints set up by the military. After they finished the beer, they stopped, snorted lines of cocaine, and purchased more beer. The men also frequented many strip clubs and received lap dances. The pattern continued as the men did more cocaine and drank more beer.

Tijuas, his speech slurred and his jaws tight from cocaine, asked Juan to drive him home. Juan agreed, and as the men were driving, a traffic officer signaled for them to stop. By this time, Tijuas was passed out, and Juan thought about killing the cop. The two soldiers that accompanied the cop stepped out of the police vehicle and trained their assault rifles on the Expedition. *Maybe killing this cop would not be such a good idea*, Juan thought. Juan removed his American license and a hundred dollar bill from his wallet.

"Good evening," the officer offered his hand to shake Juan's, and Juan extended his own hand in return.

"Evening officer. My friend is way drunk, and I am just taking him home."

"Smells like you have been drinking, too."

"Yeah, but Mr. Benjamin Franklin says that I am good to drive." Juan folded the hundred dollar bill, placed it under his license, and he handed the bribe and identification to the officer.

As the officer smoothly palmed the bill, a Cheshire cat smile emerged upon his lips. He looked at the license and returned it to Juan. "I believe you are right. Be careful."

"Thanks. I will," Juan said. If the soldiers hadn't been there, he would have killed the cop. *Lucky son of a bitch.*

Juan dragged Tijuas into his apartment, threw him on his bed, and locked the door as he left. Juan's apartment was on the other side of town, so he stopped at a nearby motel to avoid possibly encountering another traffic officer. He slept terribly, his dreams full of prison memories. When he awoke, he decided to leave the small motel room without taking a shower because he felt claustrophobic.

His head still throbbing, Juan stopped at a seafood restaurant and bought a beer prepared with tomato juice, lime, and chili. He also ordered shrimp soup, and his headache dissipated shortly thereafter. He hadn't noticed how attractive the waitress was, or how young, but he did know that he was feeling better. He flirted with her, but she was only friendly. Juan didn't care because he would have her, sooner or later, nicely or not. It would probably be sooner, and it would probably be against her will which he thought would be even better.

After arriving home, Juan sat on his bed staring at a blank wall. He was feeling anxious, so he walked out to the stairs that led from his apartment to the parking lot below, lit a cigarette, and dragged deeply. The complex was quiet because it was only at about half its capacity. It reminded him of living in the projects in California when he was young. He usually stayed away from his childhood memories, but he decided to indulge, and he let his mind drift back to the late eighties when he was still a boy.

He remembered his mother with her big hair, dark make up, and Chola tattoos on her neck, back, thigh, and right ankle. She managed a ring of girls, which were part of a larger ring, and she was in charge of distribution of crack cocaine. Juan didn't know his father. He knew many men that entered his mother's life, some who were father-like. The few times Juan had questioned his mother on the identity of his real father, she had always answered by beating him with whatever she had at hand at the moment. By the time Juan was ten, he was part of a gang, and by eleven he had committed over forty felony crimes. He tried to remember fun times, but he couldn't seem to conjure up good memories. The only thing he could recall that might have been considered fun was beating someone or smoking crack cocaine.

He thought about the girl from the massage parlor and again of the waitress. *Wonder if I can get a younger chick. Maybe back on the strip. If I could find one that would let me choke her a little, maybe beat her up, I'd gladly pay for that shit. Maybe I don't have to pay for it. Maybe I will just pick one up at a club or something.*

The final thought really excited Juan. He could train her the way he wanted. The only problem with that plan was the length of time it might take to seduce a girl.

Juan locked his apartment door and walked downstairs. He got in his Ford Expedition and drove without direction or to any specified destination. He ended up on the outskirts of town where he picked up a thin woman that was hitching a ride outside of an all-night convenience store.

"Where you headed?" Juan asked.

"I live just a ways from here, about ten minutes. Want to join me for a bit?"

Juan laughed. By the gruff voice and a few other physical indicators, he determined that she wasn't even a she. *Who the hell else would be out this late but a tranny, anyway?*

Juan deliberated between kicking the transvestite out of the car and taking her/him to her/his place to get a blow job. He opted for the blow job and followed her/his directions. After many turns and a few dirt roads, Juan arrived in a dilapidated part of town. A group of young boys, probably from nine to about fourteen years old, and one teenage girl, played outside next to the transvestite's house. The teenage girl approached the SUV and talked to the transvestite. She was high; all the kids seemed high, and they were sniffing glue from wads of toilet paper in their hands. Her lips were red and her face was flush. She was very attractive, with long black hair and brown skin, and she was wearing micro shorts which showed her thick legs. As her bloodshot eyes met Juan's, she smiled flirtatiously. Juan smiled back. When the girl stepped away, the transvestite turned to Juan.

"So, you ready to come in?"

Juan was no longer interested in the transvestite. He was staring at the young girl. "Nah. I'm out."

The transvestite frowned and opened the door of the SUV to exit the vehicle. He/she looked back one more time, hoping Juan might change his mind. But Juan had a new plan. He drove away slowly, rolling down the passenger side window as he did. The teenage girl was staring at him and waved for him to stop. Juan did, and she leaned over and put her head in the window.

"Where you going?" the girl asked.

"Drive around a while. I don't know, don't have any place to go."

"Can I drive with you?"

"Hop in."

The girl opened the passenger side door and got in the SUV. Her shorts barely covered her rear, and her legs were naturally smooth. She rambled on about the gangsters at her house. As Juan made several turns to get quickly away from the girl's house, she asked him if he had any drugs and beer.

"So was that your house?"

"Yeah."

"And your parents?"

"Asleep. Just my mother. She works really early at a factory."

A look of concern appeared on her face, a reality of what she had done and the possible situation that was forthcoming.

"You know, you better take me home. I don't feel like cruising anymore."

Juan smiled. *A little too late for that, baby*, he thought."Yeah I will take you home, don't worry, right after we pick up something from my apartment."

The girl's look of concern turned to terror, and she struggled to open the passenger door. Juan had locked the door; he previously had the door configured so that it couldn't be opened unless he unlocked it from the driver side.

Juan stopped the SUV and shut off the ignition. The houses nearby were dark, and no one was on the dirt road.

"Hey, relax, I'm not going to hurt you...*much*."

The girl's bloodshot eyes became wide with fear as she was seemingly sobering up. Juan was glad she was more sober because now it would be even more fun. Without warning, he punched her solidly in the jaw, knocking her unconscious.

Juan restarted the SUV and drove until he could not see any more houses on the road, and once again, he turned off the ignition. He awakened her, wanting to hear her scream and beg as he raped, choked, beat, and raped her again. When he was finished, she was limp like a rag doll, and bloody, but she was still alive. Juan thought about killing her, but car lights passed in front of his Ford Expedition that illuminated his face, and he decided to just leave her instead.

When the car was out of sight, Juan exited the vehicle and smoked a cigarette. The girl was motionless in the backseat, barely in an upright position with her head at a strange angle. He finished his cigarette, opened the rear door, and pulled the girl out as he let her drop to the ground. The girl moaned. Her fate would be up to whatever god she prayed to because Juan was feeling truly merciful.

Chapter Twenty

Silva was smoking a Cuban cigar; it was a real one, not the counterfeit cigars that were sold downtown to the *gringos* when they used to actually visit Juarez, Felipe remembering Silva telling him that once. Silva pushed five thousand dollars in one hundred dollar bills towards Felipe. Felipe raised his right pant leg, exposing his boot, shoved the money into the piping, and lowered the pant leg back over the boot. Silva was observing him, a smirk on his face. Felipe despised the way the lawyer looked at him. As often occurred in his meetings with Silva, Felipe's mind pondered murdering the lawyer with the .45 he carried in his shoulder holster. Felipe smiled at the thought.

"El Jefe wants this one very messy. Put his head in the monument plaza. If there is anyone with him when you do it, do the same thing to him," he said, pushing the file to Felipe. "You know, Felipe, there are at least a hundred guys that will be glad to kill for even a hundred dollars."

Felipe nodded. "Yeah. So?"

"I'm just saying. You are a lucky man, El Jefe gives you all the special projects. He's been talking about a meeting with you."

"Sounds good. When?"

"I'll let you know. Take care."

Felipe left without saying anything else. *If this arrogant son of a bitch wasn't so important to La Linea, I would have given him a Columbian necktie a long time ago*, he thought.

After their last encounter, the lawyer's secretary purposely ignored Felipe as he left the office. Felipe climbed into his truck, closed the door, turned on the dome light, and opened the file he had just received from Silva. A picture of a well-dressed cowboy was paper clipped to a document with the man's information, current address, and known hangouts. Felipe closed the file and drove home.

Ruby was cooking in the kitchen, and the smell of beef soup overcame Felipe as soon as he parked the truck. His stomach rumbled. He was still thin, but he had definitely gained weight since moving in with Ruby. Felipe opened the door and Ruby was waiting for him, a smile on her face, her arms open to hug him. He closed the door, and they hugged and kissed.

Felipe went to the bedroom and removed the cash he had stuck in his boot. Ruby was in the kitchen, and Felipe shut the door. He pulled on the floor vent, and when it gave, he stuck his arm deep inside, removing a black plastic bag. Opening the bag, he added the five thousand dollars to the fifteen thousand dollars that were already there and replaced the bag in its hiding location. He shut the vent.

Felipe returned to the kitchen, and Ruby served him a bowl of soup, steam rising from the bowl as she set it on the table. She warmed up corn tortillas on the *comal*, toasting them just the way Felipe liked. Felipe began eating.

"You going to eat?"

"I already did, my love. Enjoy."

Felipe hungrily ate two bowls of soup and six tortillas while enjoying a Tecate as well. Satisfied, he stepped outside to light a cigarette because Ruby didn't like for him to smoke in the apartment. He laughed at himself as he lit his smoke, remembering how he had always mocked other men who let their women control their actions. He understood now why they did; sex and food really tamed a man.

Felipe followed his next assigned target for a few days. It was obvious to Felipe why El Jefe wanted the man dead; he had been selling cocaine without a license. Anyone who sold illicit materials was required to have a license from La Linea, and if they didn't, it meant that they were working with or for some other cartel. Worse yet, the man previously worked for La Linea and started buying cheaper cocaine from a man with connections to La Familia Michoacana. For this reason, he had to make a show of the killing and behead him.

Felipe and Jorge, his cousin, kidnapped the cowboy directly in front of a well-known mall in Juarez at around three in the afternoon when there were many witnesses. Jorge drove right up to him as he exited the mall, and Felipe jumped out, put a gun to the man's abdomen, and pushed him into the truck. The cowboy didn't fight. The victims never did, always hoping for some small chance that the situation would appease itself and they wouldn't be killed after all. But they were foolish; when a gun is pointed in Juarez, it almost always means someone will die.

Felipe and Jorge drove the cowboy a few miles south of Juarez to an abandoned building. The structure was a concrete slab with concrete block walls and no roof as it was probably an unfinished project that had been abandoned many years ago. Tumbleweeds were stuck in the corners like homeless people huddling for warmth. The wind was blowing so hard that when Felipe opened the truck door, it shut violently on him. He opened it again with more caution and removed the cowboy, throwing him to the ground. The cowboy hadn't ceased whining since he was kidnapped.

Jorge removed a machete from the back of the pickup and walked to the cowboy, swung, and severed his head at the neck. The man's eyes remained open, framing the look of disbelief on his face forever. He finally stopped whining.

Felipe retrieved a few old blankets from the cab of the truck and threw one of them to Jorge. The men laid the blankets down on the ground next to the head and its former body. After wrapping the body in the blankets, Felipe picked up the head by its hair and wrapped it in a plastic bag from a local grocery store.

Felipe and Jorge waited at the unfinished structure until late at night, drinking beer to pass the time. When it was close to midnight, they placed the wrapped body and bagged head in the back of the pickup and returned to Juarez. El Jefe had ordered for the cowboy's head to be placed on the statue of Benito Juarez, the city's namesake, but when Felipe and Jorge drove by the monument, an olive green truck with several soldiers standing in the bed passed in the opposite direction. Felipe and Jorge continued to a gas station that was open all night, one of a very few that still remained open after nine. After filling up the tank, the men returned to the statue. Now, there wasn't anyone around, and Felipe jumped out and positioned the head on top of the statue of Benito Juarez. He returned to the truck, and the men drove to the opposite end of the city to discard the body in front of the high school that the dead cowboy had once attended.

Felipe dropped Jorge off and returned to his apartment. After he turned off the ignition, he felt uneasy for some reason as he walked to his apartment door. He pulled out his gun and held it close to him at gut level. He tried the door to the apartment without unlocking it, and it opened. It was dark. The living room looked empty. He let his eyes adjust to the darkness and walked in cautiously. There was no furniture. He went to the bedroom, and the mattress was all that remained. He turned on the light and immediately proceeded to the vent. All of his cash was gone. *Ruby!*

He quickly removed his cell phone from its case on his hip and dialed Ruby. It went directly to her voice mail. He hung up. He called her again, leaving her a message.

"Bitch, I am going to find you, and when I do, I am going to cut you into little pieces. And your mother too." He shut his cell phone and returned it to the case.

He turned on all of the lights in the apartment and searched every room for any trace of Ruby. Nothing. She had even taken the money transfer receipts that she had kept when she had sent her family money. It was as if she never existed. Felipe yelled a horrifying howl like that of a wounded beast. He pounded on the walls. He threw his mattress around. He took a knife that he carried in his boot and ripped the innocent mattress apart. He kicked the walls and doors and put holes into everything that he could. When he had exhausted himself, he fell to the floor, prostrating himself before an imaginary god or demon, his prayer for vengeance unheard. He sobbed in his hands, but he shed no actual tears. He had not been able to produce actual tears since he was a very young boy.

Felipe didn't sleep all night. He drank beer and did cocaine in place of breakfast. Later, he left in his truck and picked up Jorge because he was supposed to pay Jorge for his share of yesterday's murder of the cowboy. Felipe had five hundred dollars in his wallet. He removed the money and gave it to Jorge at a red light in an intersection. Jorge looked confused because Felipe had promised him a thousand dollars.

While waiting at the red light, a disheveled man in his late twenties began to clean Felipe's windshield with a dirty rag. Felipe waved him off, but the man ignored him. Felipe yelled for him to go away, but the man continued to ignore him. Felipe grabbed a dollar bill from inside his jacket pocket, placed it in his left hand, and stuck it out the window. He pulled his pistol from his shoulder holster with his right hand, and when the man approached for the dollar, he shot a bullet nearly between the man's eyes. The man fell to the ground and some cars ran the red light, oncoming cars' brakes screeching to avoid them. People began to crowd on the sides of the streets to see the dead man's body. The light turned green, and Felipe made a left turn. No one followed.

"Damn, you just killed that guy for cleaning your windshield!"

"He left streaks on it."

Jorge kept quiet about the other five hundred dollars that Felipe owed him.

Chapter Twenty-One

"Turn there! Turn there! Motherfucker!" Juan winced as a bullet penetrated his shoulder.

Tijuas turned sharply, and the blue Jeep Liberty which pursued them also followed. Tijuas almost lost control on the turn but regained it, and now the vehicle was gaining speed. They were still outnumbered by four people even after Juan and Tijuas had taken care of two of their attackers in front of the convenience store where they had been ambushed.

"Take a left and then turn the car and stop so we can use it as cover. Let's just fight it out before the cops join in on this party." Tijuas nodded and did as instructed, and tires screeched as they came to a sudden halt.

Juan jumped out of the car, firing with his left hand while utilizing his right hand for support. Then he crouched behind the front of the vehicle, using the engine block for cover. Apparently, the driver was not expecting Juan and Tijuas to stop, and when the Jeep Liberty approached, Juan and Tijuas easily fired and killed the driver and front seat passenger. The other two men in the back of the Jeep Liberty jeep jumped out, firing, and bullets ricocheted off the car while other rounds penetrated the thin metal of the doors.

Juan and Tijuas both screamed with rage, the heat of battle igniting their adrenaline. They returned the fire, changing out magazines as they ran out of ammunition. The firefight lasted only a minute, but for Juan it seemed like hours. When one of the two remaining attackers was hit in the leg, the other threw his weapon down and ran to escape. Juan shot at him and missed, the loss of blood from his shoulder finally taking effect. Tijuas approached the attacker with a bullet in his leg and shot him once in the head as he pleaded for his life.

"Let's get out of here, Juan."

"Truck's a mess, we'll have to hoof it."

The two men concealed their AK-47s and walked away quickly from the scene. Juan called Johnny.

"Hey, we were ambushed. Can you send someone for us? We're on-" Juan looked around for street signs, but there weren't any posted. Tijuas pointed at a small restaurant, the address on a sign near the entrance. "Place called Pollo Feliz, right off of Panamericana and Centeno."

The ten minutes that passed seemed like an eternity, and finally a white Ford Mustang pulled up next to Juan and Tijuas. The restaurant was closed, possibly because of the shooting that had just occurred around the corner. Most of the little businesses appeared to be closed, and it was only three in the afternoon. The driver waved at the men, and they entered the vehicle. Sirens penetrated the otherwise silent street, and the driver of the Mustang departed in the opposite direction of the piercing noise. He looked at Juan.

"You need a doctor?"

Juan nodded. "Probably."

"I know one we can see. He treated Johnny when he got shot last year."

The driver traveled down a series of streets, and Juan drifted in and out of sleep. Juan awoke when they arrived at a small, simple office with a sign that said "Doctor." The loss of blood had made Juan extremely groggy, and the driver and Tijuas helped him out of the car and dragged him into the clinic as a drunkard would be carried by his drinking mates.

The entrance to the small office was open, and it had been made into a tiny waiting room. The door to where the doctor saw his patients was closed, so Tijuas opened it. A woman sat in a chair in front of the doctor who sat behind a desk. They both were surprised by the sudden intrusion, and when the sight of the gunshot wound registered with the woman, she rose and left. The doctor immediately stood and pulled down the clean exam paper on the table. Tijuas and the driver helped Juan on the table, and he drifted in and out of consciousness while the doctor prepared to treat the wound.

"I don't have any anesthesia, so you'll have to bear down on this." The doctor put something plastic and rubber-like into Juan's mouth, and Juan bit down hard.

As the doctor extracted the bullet, a lifetime of painful memories was relived in Juan's head - momma's boyfriends beating him, gang fights as a youngster, and many, many fights in the *pinta*. At some point, he must have lost consciousness, because when he awoke, he was in the car again. Tijuas saw that Juan was awake and put his hand on Juan's uninjured shoulder.

"We'll be at your apartment in a few minutes."

When they arrived at the apartment, the driver and Tijuas helped Juan to his room and into his bed. They asked if he needed anything, but he said he was fine and just needed sleep. They left and Juan slept.

Juan didn't know how long he had been asleep, but he awoke incredibly thirsty and famished. His shoulder felt as if it had been hit by a truck. He sat up and became extremely dizzy. He lay down again and inched his way to the edge of the bed. His sheets were stuck to his shoulder, and he peeled them off of the blood-soaked bandage. The pain in his shoulder made him nauseous. He sat up very slowly this time and then swung his legs over the bed, but as he stood, he fell back on the bed. Cursing himself, he got on his hands and knees, placing most of the weight on his left arm and legs, and he crawled to the bathroom. He made his way to the tub and shower combination and turned on the faucet. Cool water gushed out, and Juan stuck his head in the steady stream, turned his head, and drank the water, which he vomited. He then repeated the process, and when he finally felt satiated, Juan crawled to the kitchen. Still on his hands and knees, he opened the refrigerator and pulled out left over tacos. He ate them cold, and they tasted delicious. He crawled back to his bed, took off his clothes, and went back to sleep.

Later, the incessant vibrating of his cell phone woke him up. He reached for the phone that was in his pants on a dresser near the bed, and a terrible pain shot through his shoulder and down his arm. He winced as he inched closer to the dresser and reached awkwardly for his pants. The cell phone indicated that the battery was about to expire, so he answered one of several text messages from Johnny and another from Tijuas. He was fine and would need a few weeks to recover he told them. Johnny answered his text and told him that he could send a nurse over to look after him; Juan texted him that he would let him know. He shut the cell phone off and went back to sleep, his last conscious thoughts about the facts that he would not be able to lift weights or have fun with young girls.

Chapter Twenty-Two

Felipe started drinking at four in the afternoon. He drank a beer called Indio, one after another, placing the bottles in a triangular formation like a fresh set pins in a bowling alley. His pocket was full of cash with enough money to drink for a week and still have change for a couple of whores.

However, Felipe wasn't really interested in whores. He wanted Ruby, even though she had left him. She betrayed him, but he didn't really blame her. He was ugly, a killer, and the only thing he really had going for him was a steady flow of money, and that would only be until someone else did him in. She did what was in her best interest, but he really wished she hadn't made him love her. The real betrayal was her making him feel as if he were loved by this beautiful young girl that was a great cook and even better in the bed. That was the true betrayal, the treason committed against his heart. Treason was punishable by death.

When Felipe could barely stand, or see straight, he told the wench that was the bartender to call for a cab. His mind was clear enough to realize that he could not drive in his present condition. The cab arrived, and Felipe asked the driver to take him to a hotel. The cabbie helped him out of the car and up to his room. Felipe gave him a tip, although he didn't know how much. The size of the smile on the man's face was the only gauge as to whether it was enough. It was important to him to leave good tips because he remembered all too well being poor most of his life, and he certainly didn't want to be stingy now that he had money. Felipe stumbled to the bed, clumsily pulled the covers down, and climbed in under the sheets. A drunk sleep fell upon him.

Felipe awoke just a few hours later when one of the nearby room's doors slammed shut. He always slept lightly. One never knew when hit men from El Chapo's cartel might arrive to eliminate the competition. Even when he was on the toilet, Felipe was not without a weapon, ready to unload on anyone who might attempt to attack him when he was most vulnerable.

His mouth tasted awful, and he rose from bed and went to the sink where he used the hotel's complimentary toothbrush and toothpaste. He also drank the complimentary water, and shortly thereafter vomited the water on the hotel room's carpet. His head throbbed. *Where's my truck? How did I get here?* He rummaged through his memories of the day before.

I stopped to have a beer. Downtown somewhere. On Vicente Guerrero. Felipe envisioned the outside of the bar. He remembered parking at a nearby lot and drinking at the bar, but his memories thereafter faded, other than the taxi driver helping him into the hotel room. He checked the time on his cell phone. *Six-thirty. Time to cure the hangover.* Felipe called a cab.

A few minutes later, Felipe arrived at La Choza where he ordered a *menudo.* He ate a few bites, proceeded to the bathroom to vomit, and returned to finish the *menudo.* The coffee was strong, and it had the particular taste coffee has when brewed in restaurant coffee makers. Finally, Felipe's stomach settled, he felt human again, and he could now begin the quest to find his truck.

A cab arrived at the restaurant a few minutes after he called, and he instructed the cab driver to drive to the area where he believed he had been the night before. He stopped at the parking area but could not find his truck. He grabbed the cell phone from his hip and called a cop, also with allegiance to La Linea.

"What's up, Felipe?"

"I lost my truck."

"In a roadblock?"

"No, but I think it might have been stolen."

"Ok. So do you need this official or unofficial?"

"Unofficial. My plates are HJK93F. Red Ford Lobo. Tinted windows, chrome rims."

"Yeah, I remember it. When I find it, what do you want me to do?"

"If you find it with someone in it, hold him for me. I'll give you two-fifty for finding it, four hundred if whoever has it is still in it."

"Deal."

Felipe knew that the "law" in Juarez worked hard as long as it was for the right price. He had the taxi driver take him to the hotel again. When he entered the hotel room, the bed was already made and the room smelled of pine-sol cleaner. He figured he could attempt to get some sleep while he waited for the cops to find his truck. As he lay down and rested his eyes, Felipe thought of Ruby and her fantastic ability for oral sex.

After thirty minutes without falling asleep while thinking of Ruby, Felipe was horny. He left the hotel on foot in search of a convenience store, which he found just three blocks away. He bought a Coke and a *PM*, the local yellow newspaper. In the back of the *PM*, advertisements were listed for call girls. Like many things in Juarez, prostitution was illegal but allowed. He looked through all the ads, a total of about thirty, as he walked back to the hotel. He decided upon one that read "College Girls Eager to Please 24/7," and he dialed the listed cell phone number.

"Hello?" A girl answered in a sleepy voice.

"I am at La Lucerna, room 21. How much time before you get here?"

"Give me forty minutes baby so I can get dressed up nicely for you, okay baby?"

"Sure. I'll be waiting."

Felipe hung up and turned on the TV. He found some pornography but watched it with very little interest. *This is slightly better than watching cartoons or the news*, he thought.

An hour passed, then an hour and a half, and Felipe was about to call another ad when he heard a knock on the door. He peered out the window, moving the drapes slightly aside, and he saw a young lady, probably nineteen or twenty years old, in a short skirt and a halter top. She wore her bleach-blond hair in braids, and she had extremely long fingernails. Somehow she caught a glimpse of him peering at her, and she turned her head to him and smiled. She was no Ruby, but she would suffice.

Felipe opened the door, and the call girl entered the room.

"You're late."

"Sorry, baby. It took a while to get ready, and the cab was late too."

"Whatever. Here you go." Felipe handed her sixty dollars, and she slipped the bills into her purse.

Felipe watched her undress. Her skin was tight, her breasts were natural and full, and her body was exquisite. She had a bit of a tummy, probably from a recent pregnancy. Felipe undressed and she began to caress him. She played with his penis, but Felipe was not aroused. She worked him harder, but still, no response. She gave him oral sex without a condom but to no avail.

"What's wrong, baby? What can I do?"

Felipe had never experienced this before. It seemed to him that perhaps Ruby had ruined him for other women. Maybe she had done some witchcraft on him. Whatever was wrong, it wasn't going to fix itself now, and Felipe didn't feel like enduring the humiliation. He sent the hooker on her way, and it was probably the easiest sixty dollars she had ever made. Anger filled his chest, and he thought he might explode. His mind screamed Ruby's name over and over. He fell into a troubled sleep and was dreaming that the federal police had arrived and were knocking down his door. He awoke abruptly when his cell phone rang.

"Yeah."

"I found your truck and the person who stole it."

"Great. Where are you at?"

The cop gave Felipe directions to where he was holding the thief. Felipe called a cab, splashed water on his face, and gathered his belongings. The cab arrived a few minutes later, and Felipe repeated the directions he had received earlier from the cop to the taxi driver. The driver became frustrated by Felipe's one-worded answers when he tried to initiate further conversation, and thus, they drove in silence. Prior to reaching the destination, Felipe told the cab driver to stop; he could walk the remaining blocks and ensure that the taxi driver was not a witness. Felipe turned a corner into an alley behind some abandoned buildings and was greeted by Pedro, one of many cops on La Linea's payroll.

"He's in the back of the squad car." Felipe nodded.

Felipe walked by the car as he proceeded to his truck, nodding at Pedro's partner, a tough looking female with short, black hair and a round, pudgy nose. A skinny young man with thin eyebrows sat in the rear seat of the squad car. He was noticeably nervous, but he obviously thought that he was going to jail because he didn't have the look of terror on his face that those who are about to be executed usually do.

Felipe checked his truck and made mental notes of the damages and missing possessions. He walked back to the police car, and Pedro removed the thief from the rear seat. The young man smiled nervously at Felipe, but Felipe did not return the smile. The kid was wearing some kind of pants that were just to his hips, like a girl's pants. Felipe wondered why young men plucked their eyebrows and wore hip-huggers if they weren't gay. The young man still did not realize the gravity of his current predicament.

"How old are you?"

"Seventeen." The kid smiled nervously. His hands were behind his back, tied with flexi-cuffs.

Felipe kicked the kid's legs from under him, and he fell on his side, grunting as he did. Felipe paid Pedro what he had promised and told the cops to leave. He turned around and saw that the kid had recovered his footing and was now running. Without hesitation, Felipe removed his gun and shot him in the back. He calmly walked over to the kid, who was writhing in pain and moaning on the ground, and he turned him over on his back using his booted foot.

"You should have gotten a job."

Felipe then put a bullet in the forehead of the young man. Felipe boarded his pickup and left the scene of his crime, unhurried.

Chapter Twenty-Three

Saul arrived at the scene of yet another murder, the fifth on this day, number twenty-two for the week so far, and it was barely Wednesday. A young man, who was in his late teens or early twenties and wearing hip pants and a tight t-shirt, was on the ground face up with a pool of blood under and to the side of his head. Two city cops, a male and a female, were smoking cigarettes and laughing as they guarded the scene. Saul snapped photographs from where he was standing just beyond the police tape. The male cop walked casually over to Saul and nodded his head to him.

"That guy," he said, pointing to the cadaver and taking a last drag on his almost finished cigarette, "was a known thief. It's dangerous to be a thief in Juarez."

Dangerous to be in Juarez, period, Saul thought. "Thanks. I will note that."

Saul left the scene, the image of the young man's bloody head fresh in his mind, and as he drove the streets full of traffic, he wondered if Juarez could ever change. He made some lane changes, turned, and as he did, he noticed a car following him. The car was a plain white Ford Crown Victoria. *Why are the police following me? Or maybe they aren't really police, but they want to look like police. Or maybe they are police doing some work for the mafia on their off-duty time.*

Many questions surfaced in Saul's mind, and his heart was racing. He realized his best option was to evade whoever was following him. In an effort to elude his pursuers, Saul made a turn from the outside lane, cutting off other cars in the process, and people honked angrily in response. He sped up wherever he could, but the white car managed to remain closely behind. He was in a residential area now, and he was not very familiar with the neighborhood, so he decided to return to a main road before he got trapped in a dead end.

As he turned on Lopez Mateos, the white car continued straight and disappeared from his view. His cell phone beeped to inform him of a new incoming text message. He parked at a convenience store and surveyed the area for the white car. When he was satisfied the car was no longer a threat, he read the text message.

"We know who you are fucker and we are watching, don't fuck with _____." The "_____" in the message meant La Linea.

Saul looked around again for the white car, just in case. His hands were shaking slightly from adrenaline, and he was sweating profusely. When his cell phone, still in his hand, rang, Saul jumped. The caller ID said "Mom."

"Hello Mom."

"Are you okay Mijo?"

Saul was surprised. His mother rarely called him during his work hours. "Yeah mom, I'm fine. Why do you ask?"

"I have had this terrible feeling all day. I just wanted to make sure that you were okay."

Saul was even more surprised. "Yeah mom, everything is okay. I am just heading to the office to write a story."

"Thank God and the Virgin Mary. Mijo, be careful."

"I will. Love you." Saul hung up. *Was that coincidence or a mother's instinct?*

Saul exited the car and entered the convenience store. He browsed the various drinks in the refrigerated section of the store and opted for a one and a half liter of bottled water. After paying for the water, Saul stopped at the door before exiting and surveyed the scene outside. There was no white car and no men with guns as much as he could see. He returned to his car, turned on the ignition, and opened the bottle of water. The water was cool in his dry mouth. Fine wine would not have tasted any better to him at that moment.

As he drove back to the office, he thought about his mother. She had always been a devout Catholic, but after his father died, she dedicated all of her free time to the church. She was never happy with Saul's decision to be a crime reporter, and they had heated discussions about his career choice when Calderon started his famed drug war.

Recently, Saul had written a series of articles about how only ten percent of all the arrests of cartel members in Mexico were Chapo's men, even though Chapo's cartel was the most prevalent and influential. Saul had received several threats on both his cell and house phones, and federal police had stopped him several times shortly thereafter, searching his car for "weapons." He had written about that too. His latest series was about the many arrests of Linea cartel members in Chihuahua and their subsequent acquittals because of the lack of evidence. Saul was well aware that his articles were probably unwelcome from numerous groups of people.

When he arrived at the office, Saul continued to work on his latest series about the multiple arrests of Linea cartel members. Suddenly, gunfire disrupted the process.

"Someone's shooting at the *Juarez Daily*!" an employee yelled.

Saul quickly took cover behind his desk. The gunfire lasted a few more minutes. Car alarms from vehicles parked in front of the office building were screaming in a freakish round. After the gunshots ceased, Saul cautiously walked to the window. He saw federal police tending to the wounded in front of the hotel where the federal police had been residing for the last six months. He then ran outside to speak with any officer that would oblige since the federal police were not known for such cooperation with the media.

Saul approached an officer, smoking nervously. He used the cigarette trick again.

"Wow. That was close. I thought they were attacking the *Juarez Daily*."

"No. Several armed men in two different cars ambushed one of our intelligence people. He was in an unmarked car, and they chased him all the way here. When we heard the shots, we all ran outside and started shooting at them."

"Did you get any of them?"

"I don't know. They took off."

Saul deducted from the trajectory of the bullets that whatever had hit the office and the cars in front were probably from the federal officers' weapons when they were repelling their attackers. Saul threw down his half-smoked cigarette and returned to the office. The editor, Michelle, was ranting that having federal police positioned across from the newspaper office was placing the *Juarez Daily* and its employees at an unnecessary risk. She said she would be writing an editorial for tomorrow's edition.

Saul returned to his office and Michelle followed him. He related to her what he had learned from speaking to the federal officer outside. He removed a bottle of scotch from his desk drawer which he kept for special occasions along with two plastic cups that he had saved from an office Christmas party months earlier. After pouring them both a small amount of the nerve-calming liquid, he held up a cup and offered it to Michelle.

"Medicine?"

Michelle quickly drank the shot and immediately held the cup forward so that Saul could pour her another one.

"When I get through with the editorial, I want you to edit it, okay?"

"Sure," he said.

Michelle wrote a scathing piece on how the federal police had put the newspaper office and its employees in danger, and how this was yet another example of how poorly trained officers put innocent people in harm's way. In her article, she demanded that officers be moved to another hotel. A few days after the editorial was published, they were moved, and Saul was once again amazed by the power of the media.

Chapter Twenty- Four

Juan's boss' ranch was just south of Juarez off the highway that led to the city of Chihuahua, and it was the location of his boss's brother's birthday party. Basically, just *vaqueros* were going to be there, and Juan wasn't at all interested in hanging around the cowboy type or their music; it just wasn't his style.

Juan drove through the ranch's guarded gates and saw that there were three musical groups and an entire band waiting while another group was on stage performing. He was sure that he had seen these groups on television before. He drove up to an area designated for parking and turned off his new Ford Mustang. He stayed in the car for a moment listening to a CD, a mix of rap and oldies, as the sub-woofers bumped from the trunk. He sighed, shut the music off, and got out of the car.

"Hey, Juan, come on over here!" Tijuas was wearing the garb of a cowboy and two girls accompanied him.

Tijuas and Juan shook hands, and then Tijuas grabbed a beer from an ice chest on the ground beside him and handed it to Juan. There were people gathered around such ice chests all over the ranch.

"What's up?" Juan opened the bottle of Tecate and downed half of the beer. "Am I the only one that's not *vaquero* here?"

"Looks like it, *carnal*. Not to worry, no one is gonna say shit to you. Man, glad to see you are finally all healed up."

Juan had been out of commission for over a month because of his injury, and he had only seen Tijuas twice since the shooting. Everyone at the ranch was part of Gente Nueva, Chapo Guzman's band in Juarez, but Juan still felt out of place. When a drunken cowboy bumped into him, Juan stared murderously at the cowboy, but the man was too inebriated to notice. Juan didn't want to have to kill anyone tonight.

"Relax, *carnal*. We're all friends here." Tijuas put his hand on Juan's shoulder and got closer to speak in a hushed voice. "And besides these two hotties here," he motioned to two ladies wearing miniskirts and blouses that exposed their flat stomachs, "there are more all over this place. I've never seen so many thick-legged chicks in one place."

"I've never seen so much beer in one place. Hand me another."

Soon, Juan was stumbling and slurring his speech, and the girls didn't pay him any attention. He had seen his boss, Johnny, and they hugged and exchanged pleasantries, but neither of the men was particularly interested in hanging out with the other at the moment.

Johnny's bodyguard, El Turco, was holding his two year old, bragging to everyone about the size of his kid's penis. He and the kid were wearing their best cowboy clothes with matching hats and boots. He repeatedly referred to his son as "Mini Me."

Juan was very inebriated, so he slumped down in a plastic chair and started to sleep the garbled, drunken sleep of a man that has had too much alcohol.

Suddenly, gunfire awoke Juan out of his stupor. He instinctively went to a prone firing position while removing his gun, his dazed mind barely catching up with his sub consciousness. The sounds of gunfire were replaced by women screaming and angry men barking out orders. Engines roared and tires squealed. Juan's vision cleared as his adrenaline pushed away the alcoholic cobwebs in his head, and he stood carefully and made his way to a crowd of party-goers that were standing around bloody bodies on the ground. Juan shoved his way through to the front of the crowd and saw El Turco and his son riddled with bullet wounds. Women were crying without abandonment, and Johnny was kneeling beside the body. He was saying something, quietly, and Juan strained to hear Johnny say that he would avenge El Turco and his son.

The following day, a special meeting between Juan and Johnny was held at a safe house in an upper-class neighborhood in Juarez. "We have to make statement, Juan, a hard statement. Bloody. Decapitate people. Men, women, children, write messages on their dead bodies. Find me the killers and send them straight to hell!"

Juan nodded. He became overjoyed at the thought of a killing spree, and suddenly, he was hard-hearted. Strangely, he had never been that excited about killing before; it was just a job that he enjoyed because he was good at it. But the idea of killing women, *that* turned him on.

"We know they had to have been from La Linea. Start with the city cops that are still with them. Get any information you can out of them before you kill them. Then leave them these messages I made."

He paused, and handed Juan a paper. "Post these somewhere near the bodies. If you find them with their families, kill them *all*. Kids, old people, I don't care. They have to know that we are not to be fucked with. Not ever again."

Juan left the meeting excited. With El Turco dead, Johnny needed him now more than ever, and he might be Johnny's next right hand man. Juan called several gang members of the Mexicles and Mara Salvatrucha that had been recruited by Gente Nueva. He figured he would need about ten of the most violent men he could find to do the work required, and few people in Juarez were more bloodthirsty than gang members. He loaded weapons and machetes in a stolen Ford Expedition that Johnny gave to him at the meeting. He continued to think about killing women, and again, his heart felt no compassion.

Juan started the Ford Expedition and drove to a house near downtown that served as a Mexicles safe-house. Gangsters with more tattoos than clothes guarded the door. As the guards let Juan in the safe house, they slapped his hand and hugged him, almost affectionately.

The gang members liked Juan because he had been a gang member all of his life in Los Angeles, the birthplace of the modern gang. They called him a veteran, meaning someone who had lived the gangster life and made it to middle age, an old school gangster. A three foot statue of *Santa Muerte,* or Saint Death, stood in the corner of the room on a pedestal, surrounded by bottles of tequila, cigars, and money as offerings to her. The walls were covered with graffiti, and the stereo blared gangster rap in a mixture of English and Spanish. After someone turned the music down, Juan explained the execution plan amidst hoots and hollers. His descriptions of the death and mayhem that they were to inflict upon police officers and their families excited the gang members' primal, psychotic instincts.

The plan required simultaneous actions at three different locations. Johnny wanted the rival gang to understand that they not only meant business, but that they were also well-coordinated. Juan phoned Johnny to inform him of the vehicles they planned to use and the time they would perform the executions. With this information, Johnny called his military contacts to ensure that the plot wasn't accidentally hampered by either the military or federal police.

Two of the intended victims were men who had once been part of the local police. The third intended victim was a traffic cop that was also a mid-level leader with La Linea. Juan despised the police, but he reviled traffic cops the most. He thought their sole purpose was to write meaningless tickets that served only to aggravate and annoy people rather than curbing their driving behavior. Juan's cell phone rang, and the man's voice was a contact in the traffic police he had received from Johnny.

"Yeah, what's up, *Gordo*?" Juan loved calling the cop by his nickname. He relished in the word "fatty" as it rolled over his tongue, his loathsomeness for the man evident in every word he spoke. The policeman was absolutely terrified of Juan, and thus, he did not react to Juan's discourtesy.

"Martinez is on a traffic stop on Panamericana Street, the corner of Zaragoza."

"Good job, *Gordo*, we'll take care of it from here." Juan closed his cell phone and replaced the device in the side clip of his belt.

"Let's roll!"

The men rejoiced like Satanists at a satanic party where Satan was to be the guest. They locked and loaded their weapons as they were just a few minutes away from the place they had been told Martinez would be located. Juan called the other two groups so they could all make the melee at roughly the same time. They carried signs made on canvas that were to be displayed somewhere near the bodies, a public message to Linea members that Chapo's gang was going to kill them all, and they should run and hide like the cowards that they truly were.

Juan increased speed when he saw Martinez place bribe money from the traffic stop in his shirt pocket while walking back to his motorcycle. Martinez didn't see them coming, and Juan swerved right in front of the motorcycle, tires screeching to a halt as he did. The gangsters in the Ford Expedition jumped out and fired hundreds of rounds at the cop. The traffic offender that had been stopped by Martinez nearly caused an accident as he sped away.

Juan, disappointed, didn't even bother to waste his rounds on the body of the cop that had been obliterated within seconds by his crew. He motioned to one of the gangsters, who couldn't have been more than sixteen years old, to grab the canvas sign and place it on the wall that was adjacent to the sidewalk where the dead cop now lay. People in cars that dared to pass by stared until they saw either Juan or one of the Mexicles staring back, and then they would quickly look away. The gangsters boarded the Ford Expedition and drove away without haste. Juan's cell phone rang again.

"Boss, we did it."

"Good." Juan shut the phone.

A few minutes later, Juan's cell phone rang again, and the other team leader also confirmed success. Johnny would be pleased. Juan and the gangsters returned to the house where he had met them earlier and gave them each extra cash. The gangsters were all paid a stipend for working for the mafia, but he liked to give them something extra when things went as planned. *No wonder they like me so much*, he thought.

Juan smoked some crack cocaine from a pipe that someone had offered him - just a few puffs so that he still functions normally. The gangsters were talking and bragging about the literal destruction of their enemy. When the pipe came around again, Juan took deeper drags than before. A bottle of tequila came around, too, and Juan imbibed it as well. As the day continued, he smoked more crack cocaine, and he drank more tequila. Soon day became night, and Juan was seriously impaired. *So much for not getting fucked up.*

Despite his inebriated state, Juan left the house, got in his vehicle, and slowly headed towards Juarez Street. He pulled up beside a working girl. She walked up to the window and raised her eyebrows in a flirtatious manner.

"Get in." She obeyed.

"You can go to the motel that's right around this corner," she said, pointing to the east, "it's like five dollars for twenty minutes."

"I don't like that hotel." Juan stopped the Expedition and faced the girl.

"Well, I really don't go out of this area. So where do you want to go?"

Juan smiled and punched the girl in the jaw, knocking her unconscious. He put the Expedition into drive and headed for an abandoned building he had seen earlier. His heart was overcome with hardness again as he went over in his mind all of the things that he would do to the girl before he killed her.

Chapter Twenty-Five

The two year old girl had been hit by a stray bullet. She and her mother had been standing in front of the gas station while waiting for the bus when four armed men arrived and robbed the attendants. Federal police happened by at the same moment, and the intense firefight that ensued resulted in the death of one of the assailants and an injured little girl.

Saul mournfully watched the ambulance crew as they carried her tiny body into the ambulance. She had been hit in the abdomen by a 7.62 MM bullet, and the chances of her surviving were extremely slim. Saul had seen enough of those types of wounds in the last three years to know this without asking one of the medical personnel that attended her. As he interviewed the hysterical mother who was standing nearby, Saul choked down the grief he felt for this poor woman; his throat hurt, and he felt physically ill. He kept to asking fact-finding questions only, not asking the mother how she felt, a commonly used question by Juarez reporters.

The rest of the day seemed surreal as he covered the events that played out like a crime show - bank robbery, a double execution, and extortion. In the afternoon, sitting at his desk attempting to word the story about the woman and her child, he called the clinic where the two year old girl had been taken for treatment. The girl had died. Saul could take no more, so he went to the bathroom and began to sob uncontrollably. A soft knock could be heard on the door.

"Saul, are you okay?"

It was Michelle. Saul really liked Michelle, and if he hadn't been already married to a wonderful woman, she would have been his next choice. He admired her in many ways. Mexico was not a "woman friendly" country, and machismo was prevalent everywhere to include homes, workplaces, and the government. Women had a place in Mexican society, but it certainly was not of being in charge, especially not in charge of men. Yet, Michelle was able to not only stand out among her peers, but she actually excelled to the point that even the men around her had to set aside their prejudices and recognize that she was a great editor and leader. Saul really liked that she was highly intelligent, and she had prowess which made for a dangerous and sexy combination.

"Yeah, I'm okay."

"Come on out of the bathroom. Let's talk."

"Sure. One minute, okay? Guy can't even crap out around here..."

Michelle laughed. Surely, she had heard him crying through the paper thin door of the bathroom in his office. He splashed water in his face, dried off with a few paper towels, straightened his shirt and tie, and opened the door. Michelle stood a few feet away. She wore a smart brown business suit. He had never seen her in a skirt or dress but only in a woman's business attire. Even at the Christmas party, she was very careful not to wear anything that was too sexy or revealing, and Saul was certain she did it so that her male colleagues would not look at her in any way other than completely professional.

"What's going on?"

Saul pointed to the piece he had been working on, and the cursor on the document blinked where he had left off. Michelle stood over his laptop and began reading.

"Oh God."

"Yeah. Once again, completely innocent people are killed in the drug war. Once again, a family is torn apart, and their lives will never be the same. Once again, the federal police attack without weighing the consequences of hurting innocent bystanders, and the result is this." Saul pointed to the article on the computer.

"If our police forces were trained properly, this kind of tragedy would happen less frequently. Saul, you know as well as I do that our government is not prepared to wage war on crime. By starting a full frontal attack on the drug traffickers, the only thing they have done is forced the traffickers to become more diverse. Before this war began, I honestly can't remember but maybe a few kidnappings happening, and extortion of small businesses was practically unheard of here. Now crime is rampant, and when anyone begins to rise up and question the government loud enough to actually be heard, he ends up dead."

"Jesus, Michelle, what can we do? How can we make a positive change? I can't bear the thought of one of my little girls getting a stray bullet or having to grow up in this environment."

"I don't know. I wish I had an answer. When I feel as though our paper has become nothing but a big daily crime report, I try to remember that this is the only way to really show the country and the world what is going on here. What is really happening, not the fluffed reports that the President gives on television."

"I can't get that little girl out of my mind, her little body torn apart by a stray bullet and blood soaking her tiny pink blouse." Michelle took Saul's hand. She rarely touched any of her male employees, but they had known each other a long time, and she knew that Saul was just as professional as she. She also knew that he was happily married and incapable of cheating.

"Look, Saul, take a few days off. Take a week off. You haven't been on vacation in a long time."

Saul smiled. "I have a slave driver for a boss, that's why."

Michelle gave him an admonishing scowl. "What?"

"Just kidding. You know, I think you are right. I need a break."

"I have a friend that is a travel agent. She can get you a last minute trip to Acapulco or the Cabo at a great price." Michelle grabbed a pen that was on Saul's desk and wrote a number and name down on a yellow sticky-note.

"Call her tomorrow and get the trip lined up. Get it for as soon as you can."

"Is the *Juarez Daily* springing for it?"

"Don't push your luck, Saul. Take the time, though. Get out of Juarez for a bit."

"Thanks. I will."

"Great. Now finish your damn stories so we can both go home."

Saul's family vacation week in Cabo San Lucas seemed more like a day, but getting away from the tension and violence of Juarez was a blessing for Saul and his family. He had slept better than he had in years, the sound of the ocean lulling him to sleep every night.

On his first day back to work, Saul drove to the valley just a few minutes to the east of Juarez, Valle de Guadalupe. He remembered the last time he had been out there; it was three years ago at a birthday party for one of the children of his colleague. Many city residents purchased parcels of land in the valley so as to actually have a yard, something nearly unheard of within the city limits of Juarez. The child's birthday party included a piñata, a DJ, and a taco stand in the yard. It was a very pleasant evening, and the violence of Calderon's war had barely affected their lifestyle. However, in the time that passed since the birthday party, the valley had turned into a ghost town, the residents chased away by the mafia. Houses were burned and families had been killed. This was actually the reason that Saul was there now, to cover the story of a family that had been nearly obliterated by the violence of the town.

Saul arrived at a modest home in the valley, a small family store in front of the adobe home on a half-acre of land. An old man in a wheel chair sat in front of the store and beckoned to Saul. Saul exited his car and extended his hand to the older man.

"Saul Saavedra, sir, how are you?"

"Rafael Hoyos, at your service."

The man's face looked like brown leather, and his eyes had the milky white shade of cataracts, his sadness still evident in his gaze. He had a full head of hair, a mix of gray and white. Saul had done three articles on members of the Hoyos family who had been killed over the last six months. Only three remained in the valley now - the old man, a daughter and her crippled husband, and another daughter that Saul had only heard her name mentioned on the phone.

"Just me and two daughters left here, now. They've killed seven of us. Three of my sons, two daughters, and two of my nephews. They want us all dead. This is the only land in the valley that we still own."

"Mr. Hoyos, you said it is the government that is forcing you out and killing your family?"

"Soldiers. They were the ones who picked up my three sons."

Saul remembered the incident. The Hoyos had stood outside of the federal buildings for weeks, picketing, and they had received attention from media all over Mexico. The governor had offered to "assist" them with resources and money, but they categorically denied his help and stated that they only wanted their family members returned unharmed. After weeks of pressure, the brothers finally did appear, dead. Their bodies had been obviously buried for some time but were unearthed and placed in an area where they could be found. A message was taped to one of the bodies. "The Hoyos act as look outs and anyone else who works for La Linea will die too." There was no physical proof that soldiers had picked up the men, but several people who remained anonymous told Saul that the men who picked up the Hoyos were wearing uniforms, and the vehicles that they were driving did look official.

"So I hear that the rest of the family is leaving the valley and Juarez."

"Yes, everyone but me. I was born here, on this very land, and have lived in this same house." Hoyos pointed towards the house behind him.

"I've been here for seventy years. If they are so *brave*, they can come and kill this old man in his wheel chair. Only cowards kill women, children, and old people. Make sure you print that."

"That may provoke them more."

"It might. But print it. They have already killed my reason for living. They shut down my store. They burned down our homes. I'm going blind and in a wheelchair. My daughter takes care of me, but she is diabetic and in poor health. Their killing us will just be doing us a favor. And if they don't, well, I'm not going to shut up." Hoyos pulled out a small .22 pistol from the side of his leg.

"And I won't go without a fight; I'll shoot wherever I can see their blurs when they come for us."

Saul smiled. Hoyos was serious though, and Saul was glad that he probably couldn't see his face. He quit smiling, and Hoyos continued.

"You know, one of the biggest mistakes in Mexico was letting the government disarm us, its citizens. Look around at the world; most of the world has been disarmed but not the bad guys or the government. All these countries with gun laws that don't allow their citizens to bear arms, they don't have any less crime or killings. The bad guys will always have guns. They already are criminals so why would they respect a gun law? My daughter read to me the other day an article from the Internet about a Mexican fellow that owns a jewelry store in Houston. Thieves tied up his wife and were looting the place. He shot them both, killed them, and he was shot up in the process too, but he lived. You know what the Houston police said about it?"

Saul shook his head that he did not, forgetting that the man was nearly blind. He was about to speak when the old man started again.

"They called him a hero. They didn't jail him, didn't fine him. They did what was right and called him a hero. He defended his wife and his business, and he did it with honor so yes, he's a hero. You know what would have happened to him here? He'd be in jail. Got to hand it to the *gringos,* really."

The old man had apparently finished the interview because he suddenly extended his hand. Saul extended his own hand and returned the gesture.

"Thank you, Mr. Hoyos. It was a pleasure speaking with you. If Mexico had more people like you, we wouldn't be in the situation we are in."

As Saul drove back to the office, three different text messages buzzed his cell phone. He opened the messages while waiting for a traffic light to change. *Stop investigating La Linea or die Saavedra.* He continued to the second text message. *Your family is not safe, stop investigations.* He decided to read the third message since the traffic light had not yet changed. *I love you, have a great day. And bring milk when you come home.*

The last message was from Edilia, but Saul was receiving about ten threatening messages a day similar to the first two he just read. He couldn't change his cell phone number because it would be impossible to get in touch with his contacts. Furthermore, it probably wouldn't make a difference for long anyway; if the mafia wanted your number, or your life, they could get it whenever they wanted.

Saul answered his wife's text message, and when someone honked impatiently from behind, he realized the traffic light had turned green. He continued driving, and his hands were sweating as he was wary of any cars that might be following. He never told Edilia or Michelle about the threatening text messages he was repeatedly receiving.

Prior to his vacation in Cabo San Lucas, Saul had been following a paper trail which tied municipal police, several local politicians, the state of Chihuahua's Attorney General, and the current governor all to La Linea. He had been working on the story for eight months. He retrieved photos of secret meetings and had obtained a couple of recorded cell phone calls to politicians from known mafia members. He also had been able to establish links from the local military unit to the other mafia in Juarez disputing the territory, the Chapo. However, trying to link the Chapo with the federal government would have to be done at the national level, and that was something that Saul would not be able to do without more resources and much help. If he lived long enough, he might actually be able to get the help he needed, at the international level, but his first step would be to expose the corruption at the state level.

On his way home, Saul stopped at a convenience store and bought milk as well as some chocolate chip cookies.

Since returning from his vacation, Saul had spent the last several weeks working on his big story to expose the state and local government's corruption. He had reported many stories of fallen police officers, traffic cops, and detectives as the two different mafias had both called for their obliteration.

When a call arrived on his cell phone, Saul recognized the address dictated to him by the police informant. It was *his* barber shop. *Meny*! Saul's heart raced as the informant told him there had been a shooting inside the shop and two men were dead. He didn't have specifics. Saul rushed to the barber shop, his heart thumping hard in his chest. His last conversation with Meny was still fresh in his mind.

The federal police had cordoned off the area, and traffic was moving slowly as drivers, passengers, and pedestrians attempted to see the dead bodies as they passed. Saul worked his way through the growing crowd of onlookers, and his heart sunk in his chest when he arrived at the front of the crowd. He could clearly see Meny in a bloody heap near the swivel chair where he had received a haircut many times in the last few years. Saul did his best to gather information from the federal police, who were as uncooperative and condescending as always, and he held himself together until he was complete with his work. He called Michelle on his way home for lunch.

"Hey there."

"What's up Saul?"

"A friend of mine was just killed. I don't think I can do this today. I have the notes -"

"That's okay. Send them to me. I'll take care of it. If you need tomorrow off, take it too."

"Thanks, Michelle."

Saul cried as he drove home, and Edilia opened her arms to him as soon as he entered the house. Michelle had obviously called her.

Chapter Twenty-Six

The annual rains of June were right on time. As Saul peered out the window at the downpour, he was overcome with a deep sadness. His country was deteriorating at a rapid pace. In the past few months, he had reported on an increasing number of homicides, robberies, and extortion. Many of his college classmates had either moved out of town or had plans to do so. Small businesses, stores, salons, taco stands, bars and discotheques had closed their doors as well.

Meanwhile, President Calderon obligated more troops and federal police to drive around and arrive at the scenes of crimes just in time to cordon them off. Saul himself often arrived at scenes of crimes hours before police or soldiers were present. The troops and federal police would trample the scenes while ignoring and destroying evidence. Countless surveillance cameras in areas where crimes had occurred were later found to be malfunctioning or turned in the wrong direction.

Citizens were apprehensive about leaving their homes. Saul and Edilia were afraid to take their daughters to eat or to the store. Murders were now so commonplace that one was more likely to witness a crime than not. Saul didn't want his daughters to see the horrific nature of their country. Now, the brutality was becoming personal. Meny, his barber, was shot and killed, a victim of a violent crime. Meny's only fault was he couldn't pick and choose his customers. Edilia put her hand on his shoulder.

"What's wrong, Saul?"

Saul shook his head. "Just feeling a little nostalgic. Must be the rain."

"Come here and sit down with me. I'll call the girls, and we can play Jenga."

Saul and his family played the game for a few hours as they laughed, screamed with joy, and whined of disappointment. The family fun was almost enough for Saul to forget the reality of where he lived. When they finished playing Jenga, they ate dinner and everyone went to bed early. It was still raining, and Edilia yelled for Saul to go the bedroom.

"What? What's wrong?"

"Look!" She pointed at the corner wall of their bedroom. Water ran down the wall in a slow but steady stream. A small pool of water gathered on the floor and was slowly spreading. Saul grabbed a small, plastic garbage receptacle and placed it against the wall, successfully diverting the water in the bottom of the receptacle. He grabbed his cell phone and called Angel the plumber.

"Angel? This is Saul, the reporter who - Good, glad you remember me. Listen, remember when you said that you could repair anything? I need some help with my roof. Yeah, I understand. Sure. Thanks."

"Whom did you call?"

"Remember back in the winter the drunk I brought home?"

"How could I forget?"

"Well, he is a real handyman. He said he'll give me a good deal to fix the roof, just as soon as it isn't raining."

Edilia shook her head. "Great, a drunk roofer."

Over the next week, Saul reported on three to four murders daily. The scenes included a car wash, the front of a supermarket, and near an elementary school. When he was at the school, he photographed the dead body of a man in his late twenties sprawled out on the pavement. Teachers, parents, and students lined up at the edges of the crime scene, staring at the deceased man. Bullet holes tracked the untimely death of the man, from the sidewalk to the wall bordering the school. Saul's cell phone rang, and the caller ID said "Michelle."

"Saul, get back to the office as soon as possible."

"Ok." Saul hung up, took a few more photos, and left for the Daily building.

As he drove, Saul passed several patrol cars with police who were accompanied by soldiers. Several police had been shot and killed in their patrol cars at the beginning of the year, and after President Calderon obligated troops to Juarez, they were assigned to accompany police. Additionally, the soldiers disarmed all policemen in Juarez in a supposed test to determine if any of their weapons could be linked to crimes. Once complete, the remaining policemen were administered "trustworthiness" exams to include psychological and polygraph tests. Following these results, three-fourths of the police force was fired.

Saul pulled into the Daily's employee parking area. He waved at the guard as he entered, but he knew the guard would not return the wave. He shut off the ignition, exited, and locked the vehicle. Although he felt drained, he walked briskly to the building entrance. Michelle was waiting for him in his office.

"Calderon is sending five thousand more troops and federal police to Juarez."

Saul nodded. "Great. Maybe then he means business. This crap has got to stop." Saul smiled.

Michelle shook her head. "Feeling facetious today, are you? But we'll see. In the meantime, they're arriving at the airport at five."

Saul looked at his cell phone for the current time. It was already four-thirty. "I need to get going."

Michelle nodded in agreement. "Take care of yourself, Saul."

Saul reported the story. Over the next three months, incidents involving federal police abuse of civilians increased exponentially.

"Saul, I need you to cover an incident that is happening right now," Michelle said. "How far away are you from Lopez Mateos and Simona Barba?"

"I am having dinner with the family maybe ten blocks from there. What's going on?"

"Federal police have a roadblock there. Looks like they killed a fifteen year old girl. Ruben is on his way to take the pictures."

"Can he pick me up? I am at Los Canarios."

"I will let him know."

Edilia kissed Saul goodbye and left with the girls when they had finished eating. She was used to having Saul depart on a moment's notice.

Ruben arrived, Saul got into his decrepit white Chevrolet Cavalier, and they proceeded to the roadblock. Several other reporters were already present, but the federal police confiscated their cameras and were generally abusive. As he approached, Saul was treated the same, but Ruben remained at a distance to snap photos of the federal police and reporters bickering. Suddenly, two police grabbed a reporter by his head and forced him to the ground. The police were carrying AR-15s and were very menacing, but Saul still yelled in response to their actions.

"Hey, we're reporters, not criminals! We have rights! Let that man go!"

A large policeman approached Saul, and Saul moved quickly away from him.

"Leave me alone, I'm a reporter on official business."

The cop smiled, not a nice smile, but the kind of smile a bully makes just before he is about to punch his victim. Saul did not notice another policeman standing behind him and suddenly, the man grabbed Saul in a bear hug and took him to the ground. Soon, several reporters including Saul were arrested for disturbing the peace.

In the prison holding cell, Saul chatted with the reporters that were at the scene prior to his arrival and learned that the brother of the victim had been driving the car. They were preparing for the fifteen year old girl's *quinceañera, her fifteenth birthday celebration* and were en-route to buy hamburgers when they passed the blockade. The federal police had not motioned for them to stop, and as the vehicle passed through the blockade, the police fired their firearms, killing the girl in the process. Later, Michelle posted bail for Saul.

"See you, *compadre!*" Saul shouted at the other reporter with whom he had been talking. The man smiled and waved.

"Assholes!" Michelle said in her car as she drove Saul home. She was exceptionally livid.

"Tell me about it. That's the third time this year I've been in jail."

"Bastards hide behind their badges, abuse the public, the media, steal, and kill. They are the real criminals."

"Preaching to the choir, Michelle."

Edilia was waiting at the door and squeezed Saul hard when he entered the house. She waved to Michelle as she departed. Once again, Saul felt a deep sadness for the events happening in his city and country.

Chapter Twenty-Seven

"Hello?"

"Saul. It's me, the Lic."

"Hey Lic. Wasn't sure I was going to hear from you again."

"Saul, Saul, Saul. This is just the beginning. I have something for you that is going to rock your world. It will shake your whole concept of the federal government."

"The concept that we have a bunch of corrupt, lazy sons of bitches running the country?"

"Much worse, my friend. See you at nine, same place?"

"Wouldn't miss it for anything."

Lic hung up. Saul couldn't help but wonder what the man could possibly show him that would be a surprise about the Mexican government. As he continued his day's work, he took pictures of the arriving troops and police and interviewed the general that was in charge of the Chihuahua operation. He did his tasks halfheartedly as he was dreading yet anxiously anticipating his meeting with Lic at nine o'clock in the evening.

Lic waved to Saul as he entered, and Saul proceeded to the booth where Lic was sitting. Saul noted that he must have been there a while as evidenced by a half-empty bottle of Buchanans on the table. The Lic served Saul a glass of the scotch and poured another for himself.

"Salud."

"Salud," Saul answered, as they clicked glasses.

A small laptop sat on the table. The Lic clicked on an icon and turned the laptop towards Saul. Saul's eyes widened with horror as he watched a home video.

Chapter Twenty-Eight

"You hardly slept again last night, Saul."

"Every time I close my eyes, I see that poor dead little girl's body. And then there's what my contact showed me the other night -"

Edilia waited for Saul to continue. Her silence forced him on.

"Someone had taken a video from a cell phone; it could have been from a bedroom from the look of the angle. The Mexican army stopped a newer model Ford pickup, all decked out, typical dealer truck. The driver got out with his hands over his head, and when he turned around, they gunned him down. Then two of the soldiers walked over to him and checked for vitals. They had just sprayed him with like thirty bullets from their AR-15s, and they still wanted to make sure the guy was dead! One of the soldiers searched the truck and pulled out an AK-47 and placed it next to the body of the man. As I watched the scene, I realized that I had covered this same report not but two months ago. The soldiers had said that the man had opened fire on them first."

"Oh my God."

Edilia closed her eyes tightly, as if by doing so she could make the whole terrible incident disappear. She opened them again, and she saw her husband's haggard face and the dark circles under his eyes, and she knew everything had just changed for the worse. If citizens could not trust the government's strong arm, the one supposedly incorruptible entity in the system, what chances did Mexican citizens have of reestablishing a normal and peaceful existence?

Edilia served her husband breakfast, but Saul barely ate. She sensed there was more he wasn't telling her. She sat down in the chair beside him and picked up his right hand and held it between both of hers. She kissed his hand.

"Honey, talk to me. I have always supported your decisions one hundred percent. All I have ever asked is that you keep me involved. What is it that you're not telling me?"

Saul sighed as he stared down at his plate, the eggs and chorizo offering no help with the matter.

"A few days ago someone called me on my cell. I didn't recognize his voice, but his accent indicated he was from the Sinaloa region." He paused and turned to look into Edilia's eyes.

"He told me to back off the stories about the mafia unless I wanted to join my ancestors very soon. I got some threatening text messages, too."

Edilia gasped and felt suddenly faint. She took a deep breath and regained her composure. "Saul, this is very serious. We need you. Your family needs you. You have to let this one go. No story is worth your life, not to us."

"Edilia, I can't just let this go. This is more than a story; this is a government defrauding its people. An entity that insists that all of its citizens pay taxes and abide by the law, yet refuses to provide them with the most basic necessities of security and peace. I will write the story. We can go to El Paso for a time, until things cool down a bit. But I can't keep quiet. If we all just keep quiet, bow our heads down and just take whatever comes like sheep, it makes us just as guilty as the criminals and the government that commit the atrocities. Our children need me, yes, you need me, I know, but what good am I if I don't stand up for what is right? What kind of world will I be leaving for our children?"

"But it isn't all up to you, Saul, you are not God. You can't change it all by yourself."

"No, I can't. But change has to start with someone." He packed up his laptop and went to the office to write.

El Paso, Texas, is considered one of the safest cities in America, yet it has but a river and a fence between it and the homicide capital of the Americas, Ciudad Juarez, affectionately known as Juaritos by long- time residents. A drug war fought by both countries resulted in little progress on either side but with terrible consequences for us Mexicans, for us Juarenses especially. The major difference is the two different governments, both democracies, but one that has been and continues to be run by greed and blatant corruption. The president of Mexico jumped into a war that cannot be won, with a strategy poorly devised and more poorly implemented. The states of Tamaulipas and Chihuahua have been hit the worst by rampant crime set off by a war over the plazas, the territories disputed by the different drug cartels. Perhaps you, as I did, believe that the government is impartially fighting against all of the cartels equally, despite the apparent contrary evidence. Perhaps you know better. I will get to that.

For some, Juarez, the plaza that had been ruled by the Linea for thirty years, is their birth home. For others, it is their unfortunate new home, far from the peaceful towns they left in Veracruz, Durango, and Michoacán. But for me, Juarez is much more than just some terrible place where law and order are non-existent, where executions are a daily event, and where armed robbery is commonplace. It is still the Juarez of my childhood memories with the parks full of people on the weekends playing with their children. It was a marketplace of a collage of colors and smells, from fresh fruits and vegetables to piñatas. It was a place where neighbors band together to help one another in difficult times, where a stranger was a potential friend, and where doors were open to all.

My fellow people of Juarez, whether you were born and reared here or are a transplant from some other place in the world, we have been defrauded by our government. We are expected to believe wholeheartedly in them, obliged to pay for their supposed war against drugs, and God forbid that someone speak out against them. They demand and demand, and yet when we demand the most basic necessity of life, a secure place to live and rear our children, our cries fall on deaf ears.

Perhaps there are those of you that still believe in the government. Sometimes change is painful, I have heard it said. Maybe you have not yet been touched by the terrible crimes that occur daily within our city. Perhaps you live in a bubble. My statements are hard, true, but they are not without foundation. A video was sent to me....

Saul finished the story, proofread it, and delivered it to Michelle's box for final review. She was at lunch. Some of the other reporters invited him to lunch, but he politely declined. His head throbbed, and he seemed to feel the weight of the world on his shoulders. His cell phone rang, and he looked at the number. It was Edilia, and he answered.

"You okay?"

"Yeah. I wrote the story. You need to start packing. I will clear it with the editor later, and we can leave tomorrow, before this is published."

"I talked to my sister. She said we can stay with her as long as we want."

"Yeah, I bet. That way she can spoil the hell out of the girls every day instead of just once in a while as she does now."

"What do you expect? Her son is all grown up now."

"Well, it may be good to change our surroundings for a time. We can take the girls to the zoo and the amusement park. It will be like a

146

mini-vacation. Pack the basics. We can send for the rest later if needed."

"Okay love. When are you coming home?"

"In a bit. I'm just going to wait for Michelle."

"Eat something. I know you haven't eaten yet, and you ate very little this morning."

"I will."

"Promise?"

"Promise."

Saul waited several hours for Michelle to return. It was nearly five when he decided to call her.

"Hey, everything okay? There's lots of work for you here, and no one else wants to do it. Unless you want to give me a raise?"

"Saul, you wouldn't want my job and you know it. I got tied up after lunch at city hall with the mayor."

"Couldn't find any better company, eh? That's just as bad as spending your afternoon with a group of lawyers."

Michelle laughed. "I know. I'm on my way."

"I feel like crap. Tell you what, just read the story I left for you in the inbox. I'll see you tomorrow in the morning. We will need to talk."

"That bad?"

"Very bad."

"Okay, we can talk tomorrow. I'm going to have a long night, so don't expect me too early."

"No problem. Bye."

Saul cautiously drove home. He expected someone to pull up beside his vehicle and execute him at any moment. He was sweating at every stoplight, anxious for the red light to turn green in order to have half a chance to escape if he needed to. Finally, he arrived home without incident.

Edilia and the girls greeted Saul at the door with hugs and kisses. Everyone had been worried. After dinner, Saul read part of *Moby Dick* to the girls. He always read classics to the girls at bed time. The girls went to bed, and Saul and Edilia made love. Afterwards, they talked, Edilia resting in Saul's arms.

"When will we leave?"

"I'm not sure. I'll call you tomorrow after I speak with Michelle. She may not even want to publish it."

"She won't want to, but she will. We will have to go before that."

"Okay, baby. I love you."

Edilia planted a long, passionate kiss on Saul's lips. They fell asleep, and Saul finally slept without nightmares. It was the first good night of sleep that he had since his vacation.

When Edilia awoke, Saul was already up and at the computer. He turned to see her awake and turned back to the screen.

"I can't believe this. Can't fucking believe it."

Edilia was surprised. Saul rarely used foul language. "Can't believe what?"

"Someone must have pulled my story from Michelle's inbox. She sent me an email last night that there was nothing in her inbox from me."

"Jesus. Saul, that means -"

"Yeah. There has to be someone at the office that is working for the mafia."

"What are we going to do?"

"Get the girls packed up and ready to go. I am going to head over to the office and talk to Michelle. I already rewrote the story and emailed it to her."

"Okay. You want breakfast?"

"No, not hungry at all."

Edilia watched him as he got ready. She had a terrible feeling in the pit of her stomach.

"Saul, do you really need to go to the office today? I mean, you already emailed the story. Why don't we just leave?"

"I have to take this video disc to the office. It is the proof that she will need to print the story and to be able to deal with the aftershock. I'll go and come right back. Promise."

"Okay, but please be careful."

They hugged and kissed before he left. The disc was in his portfolio. Angel arrived just as Saul was opening the garage.

"Morning Saul."

"Morning! Say, do you think you can finish the job up by this afternoon?"

"I can try. Why?"

"We are going to probably take a trip tomorrow, and I'm not sure when we will be back. Just want to make sure the roof is good before we go, and we can settle up."

"Not to worry, Saul. If I don't finish, I can continue even if you all leave. Just pay me what you can, and if you need time, I can leave my bank account number with your wife."

"Good idea. OK, see you later."

Angel went to the side of the house and grabbed a ladder. Edilia was waiting at the garage door while Saul got into the car, started it, and put the car in reverse. Suddenly, a gray Dodge Ram pickup truck turned hard around the corner, tires squealing. Angel turned to see what was happening. Edilia's mouth opened, a scream erupting from her throat. The pickup stopped directly behind Saul's car, blocking any possible escape. Two men jumped out from the passenger side, AK-47s in hand, and lowered the barrels at Saul. One man was dressed in jeans, boots, and a western straw hat while his accomplice had a shaved head and wore baggy pants and a long sleeve shirt.

Saul remained in the driver's seat and did not attempt to move. He focused on Edilia, his eyes filled with sadness. He mouthed "I love you" to Edilia, but she was paralyzed by the situation and could only muster a nod of her head in return. Angel yelled, and he ran towards Saul's attackers. The men raised their AK-47s.

Suddenly, bullets ripped through Saul's compact car, and the tires exploded, glass shattered, and holes punched through the metal as if it were paper. Saul's body convulsed as 7.62 mm bullets destroyed his body, blood splashing on the windshield. Angel fell by stray bullets as he rushed to help Saul.

The events seemed to occur in slow motion for Edilia, and a wave of nausea mixed with impotence overtook her as she fell to her knees. Exhausted both physically and mentally, she no longer had the power to scream, and the executioners hurriedly returned to their pickup to escape, tires squealing again. Edilia was motionless except for her hands that shook violently. After a moment, she tried to stand, but she still had no strength in her legs. Her daughters ran down the stairs.

"Daddy! Daddy! No!"

Edilia tried to stop them when they ran past her, but she was powerless and could only watch her daughters as they cried and hugged the broken, lifeless body of their father. After mustering strength, Edilia walked weakly to her daughters and pried them off of their father. She retrieved the portfolio from the passenger side of the car, and they returned inside the house. Angel crawled to the garage, one of his legs bleeding profusely. Edilia heard sirens in the background as her daughters cried uncontrollably.

Chapter Twenty-Nine

Michelle wore no makeup, and her hair was simply pulled back in a bun. She was dressed in a black suit jacket with a white blouse, and she wore a black ribbon tied to her left arm.

"Saul Saavedra was much more to me and to the people at the *Juarez Daily*; he was a friend, a confidant, an example for all of us to follow. As recently graduated students, journalists in general are idealistic, and we want to change the world. The pen is mightier than the sword. Even after nearly twenty years of journalism, Saul still believed in this principle. He was an idealist. He was heart-broken over what has happened to our city, our state, and our nation, and no matter how much he was threatened, intimidated by law enforcement, mafia, and politicians, Saul was steadfast in his convictions. Saul once told me that if every person in the city did not back down when facing criminals, be it corrupt officials or otherwise, that the city would change no matter how ineffective the government. He contended that people would lose their lives in the process, but in the long run we could leave our children a better world. It was that kind of selfless thinking that defined Saul. When the threats had started, I offered to help him immigrate to the United States, and he told me that running away was no way to solve a problem. Saul asserted that Mexico needs people to stay and fight. Whoever killed Saul did a terrible injustice to his family, to our city, and to our entire nation because they murdered a true patriot and a great man."

Tears ran down Michelle's cheeks as she finished her eulogy. She walked away from the podium, and as she returned to her seat in the

San Lorenzo church, she stopped in front of Edilia and hugged her fiercely. Edilia was dry-eyed and stoic, but she returned the embrace.

Edilia rose and walked to the podium. She looked around at the silent crowd; the church's pews were filled, and there were people standing in the back. Dark circles appeared below her eyes. Her hair was black, without its usual shine, and Michelle noticed that her blouse was buttoned incorrectly, as if she had missed a button when she had dressed.

"Saul," she started, her voice slightly broken, "was easily the best man I have ever known. I could relate to you anecdotes that would make you smile, laugh, and cry, but I have no humor at this moment. A great part of my life's joy has been taken from me and my daughters, and now I must bury the man who made me a whole person. Thank you all for coming and paying respects to my husband." Edilia returned to her seat in the front pew.

Tears ran more freely down Michelle's face; she wanted to stop crying, but she was no longer in control of the sadness that had steadily grown as Edilia spoke. She couldn't refrain from staring at Saul's girls and thinking about how dreadful it must be for them. It was bad enough losing a parent, but it was worse to lose a *good* parent. She had seen Saul with his family at various *Juarez Daily's* events, and it was obvious that he was a great father. Michelle's father had been at best a distracted parent, his work always taking priority over his family. However, when he died while she was in college, it was devastating for her. Saul's daughters were young girls with a strong nexus to their father. Her mournfulness turned to rage as she thought about their loss.

With a white lily in her hand, Edilia stood over the grave of her husband, and she was unable to shed any more tears. Anger replaced the sadness she felt, and vengeance replaced the loneliness. She spoke to Saul, quietly, whispering as a lover would, but the tone of her voice was not of grief.

"Saul, you were a good man, the best I have ever known. No matter what it takes, no matter what price I have to pay, *your death will not be in vain.*" Her hands were balled into fists.

Edilia placed the lily on Saul's headstone. She walked away from the grave with a steady stride, the type that only one with purpose possesses. The wind blew her long, black hair toward the south, the whistling sound a screaming choir of the dead in her ears. They screamed for justice as well, as her husband had. They would have their justice, even if it meant that she would have to join them.

Edilia's daughters had been in El Paso with her sister since the funeral. She had no reason to bring them back to Juarez until she finished what she set out to accomplish. Her sister pleaded with her not to return to Juarez, but Edilia answered with a solemn stare that ensured that she would not beg again. She had no guns, no political power, only her broken heart and a video of the Mexican military killing an apparently unarmed man.

She had spoken with Michelle and was devastated to discover that Michelle had not even received the last story that Saul had written and sent by email. Surely, the government had somehow been able to intercept the email. Edilia's only allies were the media and the citizens of Juarez, but those resources were limited. She figured her first step was to make multiple copies of the video. Then she would visit the head of the military in Juarez who had just been transferred there a week ago to replace the other General whom Saul believed to be extremely corrupt. Hopefully, she could visit him before he also became corrupt, if it weren't already too late.

Edilia scheduled an appointment with the new General, and she took one of the many duplicated videos with her to the meeting. She also left one copy at her sister's house, and Edilia told her that if anything happened to her, she was to make sure the video was posted on the Internet.

Edilia was nervous as she waited in the reception area to meet the General. The phone rang on the secretary's desk, and an attractive young girl in her twenties answered. "Yes, I will. Yes sir." She hung up the phone and looked at Edilia. "You may see the General now."

She opened the olive-drab painted door to the General's office, his name plate shiny with black letters that spelled Molina. A man in his sixties rose as she entered, and he extended his hand and returned the gesture, shaking it briefly. He motioned for her to sit down.

"My sincerest condolences, Mrs. Saavedra. We are doing everything in our power to find your husband's killers."

"Um, yes. Right. Thank you. I am actually here on another matter, though."

The General inquisitively raised his graying bushy eyebrows. Edilia removed the video from her purse and handed it to him. As the General accepted the CD, he looked at the disc as if it were some kind of alien technology.

"It has a video on it, taken from someone's cell phone, of soldiers killing an unarmed man. It was an event that my husband was investigating before he was murdered."

The General placed the CD in a desk drawer and closed it immediately. He looked at Edilia who was leering at him.

"I will look at it later. I am not good with computers. I promise you I will get to the bottom of whatever wrongdoing there may be. You have my word as an officer and a man."

"Thank you." Edilia's facial expression showed her apparent lack of enthusiasm. She stood and left without speaking another word.

"Ma'am?"

Edilia stopped and half-turned around. "Yes General?"

"You have children?"

"Yes. Why?"

"Consider them before you continue with this. If they killed your husband for whatever is on here, then my advice would be to destroy it. Leave what you have with me, but if you have any other copies, if you have any of your husband's investigations, get rid of all of them for your children's sake." Goosebumps covered Edilia's arms as she turned back around without saying anything else.

When Edilia left the office, General Molina removed the video disc from his desk and placed it into the computer. After watching the footage, he picked up his phone and dialed.

"Sir? This is Molina. Sorry to disturb you, but we have a problem. Yes, I am on the secure line. The wife of the reporter that was killed last week came to see me. She has a copy of the video that we needed. Yes, I understand. I will take care of it at any cost. Yes sir, there will be no loose ends." The General hung up.

He looked at his thick military watch and placed a call to his secretary and ordered her to call in Captain Alanis. After about ten minutes, the young Captain arrived.

"Yes sir?" he said, saluting. The General saluted back.

"Close the door and sit down, Alanis." The Captain obeyed.

"I need intelligence on a woman. All informal, no reports other than verbal, to me only. She is the wife of that journalist that was executed. She has important information that can hurt our operation here and the government of Mexico."

The General handed the Captain the CD. "Watch it... you're in it. Then destroy it."

"Yes sir."

"Listen, I can't stress enough how important this mission is. You must ensure that you know everyone that she knows and go everywhere that she goes, including if she goes to the United States. You will be in civilian attire and will have no other duties until otherwise ordered."

"Yes sir."

"I need you to search her house, too. However you can, just make sure it happens when she is not around, and when you find what we need, computers, CDs, papers, take it all and make it look like a robbery."

"Understood."

"Carry on." The soldier left, and the General slouched down in his chair and sighed.

Chapter Thirty

"Edilia, they are in my house, they want to take my boy! They already have his friend!"

"Calm down, slow down. Who wants to take your son?"

"Soldiers. He is only seventeen!"

"I'm on my way."

Edilia hustled out the back door and swung open the garage door. Angel was outside attaching some iron bars onto a window.

"Edilia?" He asked, taking his work gloves off as he walked towards her.

"Angel, a friend needs my help. You can stay if you want."

"I'd like to go with you, if that's okay."

Edilia shrugged, and Angel closed the garage door, locked it, and entered the car with her. She drove hurriedly to her friend's home. For the last six months after Saul had been killed, Edilia had been working as an activist against the Mexican military. After her visit with the local General, her house had been robbed, and all the documents and work of Saul's investigations had disappeared. The military often removed people from their homes, and they were never to be seen again. She had never received any response from the General, and she hadn't released the incriminating video publicly. The video was what she believed was keeping her alive, and the only existing copy under her control was with her sister. Her new friend, Evelyn, was one of many new friends she had made while peacefully protesting the military's presence in Juarez.

When Edilia and Angel arrived at Evelyn's house, two olive-drab colored trucks were parked outside, and there were soldiers on the corners of the streets and at the open front door of her house. While her heart pounded in her chest, Edilia stormed right past the two guards and entered the house. It was a nightmarish scene; soldiers dragged a teenage boy out of his room, and Evelyn blocked their passage with her entire body, her corpulent stature making it difficult for the soldiers to pass through the narrow hallway. Edilia and Angel joined to help as they placed their backs to Evelyn's so that the soldiers could not push Evelyn so easily.

"Where is your warrant?" Edilia questioned.

A dark skinned soldier suddenly was in front of her, pointing at his 9mm sidearm, meaning that he didn't need any such warrant. "Stand aside or you'll get hurt."

Edilia didn't move. The soldier grabbed her right wrist and twisted, and a moment later, Edilia was uncomfortably restrained as the man had her under his control. He pushed her down to the floor and then immediately grabbed Evelyn, restraining her in a similar manner. Angel jumped forward to help and another soldier hit him in the head with the stock of his rifle. The soldiers then threw the boy in the back of one of the olive colored trucks where his friend was restrained already. As abruptly as the soldiers had arrived, they disappeared.

"Edilia, quick!"

Edilia jumped to her feet and helped Angel up. A red bump appeared just above his right temple.

"You okay?"

"Yeah, no problem. Let's go!"

Edilia, Angel, and Evelyn ran to Edilia's car and attempted to follow the two military trucks. Evelyn called her relatives while Edilia navigated the traffic. The soldiers were soon out of sight, and she couldn't get past the traffic. They were headed south, out of the city limits.

"They are headed out to the desert. I know it."

"Then let's go out there too."

Edilia drove and followed the highway that led to the outskirts of town. A few minutes later, they spotted a dirt road that had a dust cloud leading out towards the south. As they followed the dust clouds around a series of curves and hills, their hearts sank when they saw two bodies on the side of the road. Edilia stopped the car.

One of the bodies on the road was the friend of her son. Edilia placed two fingers on the side of his neck but felt no pulse. Evelyn's son was adjacent to him with his face down in the dirt. Edilia immediately thought of Saul and his lifeless body and the pain it caused her, and she shuddered. Evelyn's son moved his arm ever so slightly.

"Jose!"

Evelyn rushed to his side and began to examine his very bloody and injured body. He half-opened one very swollen eye. Evelyn's relatives began to arrive, and many were shouting angrily at the army hummer that was also just arriving. A relative handed Evelyn a blanket, and she attempted to cover Jose. Edilia and a few other relatives assisted Evelyn as they carried her son to a relative's minivan.

Edilia took the driver of the minivan by his hand. "Can you get him to El Paso? He will be safe there."

The man nodded his head, and Edilia retracted her hand. The soldiers drove by without stopping. Angel looked as if he were in shock. Edilia stared down at the other boy, and her heart sunk with anguish and impotence.

Edilia realized that the video she possessed was dangerous to everyone, including her sister. Her plan had been to deliver it to Michelle, but involving more people would mean more innocent victims for which she did not want to be responsible. Michelle had already done a considerable amount for her; she organized an extensive press conference with international media about what had happened to Saul, she insured Edilia and the girls, and she was generally just very supportive. Edilia knew that Michelle would print the story and publicize the video if she gave it to her, but the consequences would be deadly. The depth of the involvement the military had with the mafia could not be underestimated.

Chapter Thirty-One

Felipe still couldn't believe that Ruby actually called him. He thought she was going to ask for money so she could return to Juarez, but he was surprised when she asked if he could meet her at the very motel where they first met. He drove there, knowing full well that it could be a trap, but he couldn't resist. With Chapo's gang killing La Linea members everywhere, he knew this was a stupid move, but he continued driving. As he approached the motel, he surveyed the area for danger - cars with several men, police, soldiers, anything. He didn't see anything unusual or suspicious. If this weren't a trap, then Ruby had nerve for wanting to see him after what she had done.

Felipe parked outside the motel and walked to the room she had told him that she was in. The shades were closed, and the garage door was open. He closed the garage door and removed his 9mm Glock handgun, holding it in front of him. He went to the side of the door and knocked.

"Come in." It was Ruby's voice.

With his pistol still in front of him, Felipe turned the door knob, pushed the door open slightly, and then used his foot to open it completely. He saw Ruby, dressed only in a bra and panties, lying on the bed, and he went to the bathroom to ensure she was not accompanied. He stuck the pistol in his pants at the waist, the handle accessible from just under his shirt.

He approached Ruby and was excited to see her again, but he was angry at the same time. He wanted to have sex with her as much as he wanted to strangle her. Perhaps he would do both at the same time.

"Felipe, forgive me. Let me explain."

Felipe grabbed her by the throat. She was shaking, and her skin was full of goose bumps. He tightened his grip slightly.

"Please, Felipe, just let me explain." Her voice was warped, forced out through the smaller space made by his gripping hand. He relaxed his grip, but he kept his hand on her throat.

"Soldiers came to the apartment the day I left. They came, and they searched the entire apartment. They found the money, and they took it. They took everything we owned. They were asking me all kinds of questions, but I told them that I was the cleaning lady, that I barely had met my employer. I told them that I wouldn't say anything about the money if they would just let me leave. I was scared, Felipe. I sold the cell you had given me and went to Veracruz. I wasn't ever going to come back. I knew that you would be mad and wouldn't know what had happened."

Felipe studied her face. He believed her. He wanted to believe her. He wanted her, period. She pulled forward to him, kissed him, and he responded. She unbuttoned and removed his shirt. He pulled off his jeans. She reached down to touch his penis, and he was happy to feel her touch again. They had sex several times over - on the bed, on the floor, on the easy chair, and in the shower. Felipe's cell phone rang and he ignored it, something he rarely did. They had room service bring them food and beer, and after they ate, they drank and had sex again. Felipe slept better than he had in years; he still had nightmares, but with less intensity than normal, and no insomnia. His cell phone awoke him around six in the morning the following day.

"Felipe! Where the hell have you been?"

"Sick. What's going on?"

"Shit is going down. Martinez, Pablo, and Rios were all killed yesterday. Chapo left messages for us, too. El Jefe wants to see you, in person."

Felipe was not prepared for this, but he knew that the Lic couldn't be ignored. If the main boss wanted to meet him, that meant now, not later. "Okay. Time and place?"

"Meet me at the office. You can follow me to the meeting point."

"See you in thirty minutes." Felipe closed his cell phone and opened the curtains.

"Ruby, wake up."

She opened her eyes, and she squinted as the bright sunlight flooded the room.

"I have a meeting."

"Don't leave me here, please."

"It is really important. I can't be seen with you right now. They will think that I don't take them seriously."

"I'll hide in the truck. I can fit on the floor if I curl up."

"What if they want to go somewhere with me?"

"Tell them there's blood on the seat. Tell them you can follow them. I don't want you to leave me here."

"Oh, fuck it then. Get dressed quickly."

Ruby smiled and jumped out of bed. She was dressed and had her hair pulled back in a bun within five minutes. Felipe couldn't remember ever seeing a girl get ready so quickly. They got in his truck, her backpack with clothes in the middle seat. She was still smiling with a joyous, childlike expression on her face. Felipe shook his head as he questioned his judgment. He drove to the lawyer's office quickly, purposely avoiding areas of heavy traffic.

"We're here."

Ruby curled up on the floorboard of the passenger side of the truck. Felipe was about to exit his truck when he saw that the Lic was already leaving the building. The Lic acknowledged that he saw Felipe and walked to his own car. Felipe followed him until he stopped at a restaurant called El Chaparral. They both parked and went inside.

A short man with a mustache dressed in old jeans and leather sandals stood and greeted the Lic. They hugged, and the man patted hard on the lawyer's back. Another man, tall with a light complexion, extended his hand to the Lic, and they shook hands. The Lic turned around to face Felipe without giving his back to the other two men. Felipe had imagined a place filled with bodyguards, but other than the waiters and cook, no one else was in the restaurant.

"Felipe, this is the boss." Felipe extended his hand, and the short man grabbed it with both his hands, shaking it vigorously.

"And this is Rogelio. He is Mr. Baeza's right hand man."

Felipe held out his hand again. Rogelio's grip was like iron. He was a few inches taller than Felipe with a barrel chest and thick arms. He was grinning, a boyish smile that was genuine and disarming, and unable to resist, Felipe smiled back.

"Sit down, Felipe." Baeza waved to one of the waiters, and the man nearly ran to the table.

"Yes sir!"

"Bring us a bucket of Negras."

"Negra Modelo. Right away!"

"Hey!"

The waiter came to a sudden halt and turned around with beads of sweat on his forehead rolling down to his eyes, causing him to squint.

"Make sure that they are ice cold."

"Yes sir, of course." He turned back again, seemingly relieved, and he walked behind the bar.

"Felipe, the Lic has always spoken very highly of you. I was very pleased when he said that you would become a part of our team. This is official, then. You will only work for us, correct?"

"Yes sir."

"Good. I need you to work closely with Rogelio. He is going to be handling most of this, uh, situation we have right now with El Chapo and the government. He has some great ideas on how we can make an impression on the government so that maybe they will reconsider backing Chapo." He paused, contemplating Felipe for a moment, then continued. "We will be going after soldiers, politicians, and other *important* people."

"I understand."

The waiter reappeared with a tin bucket filled with eight beers and ice. Baeza motioned for Felipe to grab one, and the waiter removed a beer and opened it for him. He did the same for the other three men as well. Rogelio, still smiling, spoke.

"Felipe, we need to make a hit today. As you know, Chapo executed three important people in our organization. We need to retaliate immediately and show them that we are not afraid. They will be expecting us to hit one of their top local guys. Since they will expect it, it will be difficult."

Felipe nodded in agreement and Rogelio continued. "I already have someone in mind. He works for El Chapo, but he isn't really a top man. But he is definitely important to them. He's the new Director of Security."

Felipe frowned. This was a man that drove around in bullet-proof cars with armed security in front and back of his vehicles all the time. Rogelio smiled again, seemingly seeing Felipe's concern.

"I have it all planned out. This morning his armored SUV is in the shop. He'll be headed over for lunch with the Mayor just after noon. I have his route on this map."

Rogelio removed a folded paper from his shirt pocket and handed it to Felipe. "This is an opportunity that we may not get again. Tell me what you need, and you can have it. But I need you to move on this now."

Felipe opened the folded map. Rogelio pointed to a section right before the American Consulate in Juarez. "I suggest you hit him here. There is road construction right in front of the direction they'll be headed in, so they won't be able to move forward or backward if you hit them as they get into the traffic jam. To the west is a cement wall where you all can set up and drive south afterward."

Rogelio then used his finger to show the exact location, "To the east, this building blocks any exit. You'll have them boxed in."

Baeza removed a stack of hundred dollar bills, placed the bills on the table, and pushed them towards Felipe.

"Ten thousand now, ten when you finish the job. There will be some other things I will have you do as well, but they are not nearly as complicated."

Felipe pocketed the money and the map, stood up, and shook the men's' hands. "I will need to get started right now if I am to be ready on time."

Rogelio stood as well. "Of course. Let me accompany you."

The two men exited the restaurant, and Rogelio guided him to an extended cab Ford Lobo with a dust cover on the bed. Rogelio lifted the dust cover and removed a wooden crate filled with grenades. He then followed Felipe to his pickup and placed them in the bed of his truck. Felipe covered the grenades with one of the old blankets he used for bodies. As Rogelio passed the passenger side of the truck, he saw something in the window and smiled. He turned and winked at Felipe.

"Good luck, Felipe. My cell number is on the back of the map. Call me when you are finished with the job."

"I will."

Felipe entered the truck and turned the ignition. Ruby was silent until they pulled out of the parking lot. She popped up and sat next to Felipe, moving her back pack over so that she could sit in the middle.

"That guy saw you."

"What guy? I didn't move."

"I know. I don't know how, but he saw you. I don't think it's going to be a problem, though."

"That's good."

"You have to go. I have work."

"Take me with you."

"What? Are you crazy? You know what I do."

"Yes. Take me with you. I can help."

Felipe shook his head. "You don't even know how to shoot a gun, do you?"

"Not yet. You can show me. I want to help."

Felipe rubbed his forehead with his hand. "What the hell am I going to do with you, Ruby? What I am about to do is very dangerous, and I have to pick up some more guys. This isn't going to be a regular hit. Tell you what, if you're serious about this, let it be the next one. I don't have time at all today, and this guy is going to be heavily guarded."

Ruby frowned. "You promise it will be next time?"

"I promise. I need to do this one alone."

"Okay. Drop me off at the mall, then. I'll wait for you."

Felipe called Jorge's cell phone and told him to meet him at the Plaza Rio Grande Mall. Before exiting the truck at the mall, Ruby hugged and kissed Felipe and left her backpack in the seat. He gave her a hundred dollar bill and watched her as she walked towards the entrance of the mall, marveling at the perfect way she swayed with each step. He wondered about her reasoning for want to help him.

Jorge pulled up beside Felipe's truck and rolled down his window. Felipe motioned for Jorge to follow him, and he turned around behind Felipe's vehicle. They drove out to the area of the parking lot that was farthest from the street. After parking, Jorge boarded Felipe's truck. The men shook hands and both lit cigarettes. Felipe showed the map to Jorge as he discussed the execution plan.

"I need you to pick up ten of the meanest fuckers you know. Don't tell them shit except what they need to know, not who it is or anything like that. Make sure they know that they have to kill the cops that are around. None of the cops that are guarding this guy can be left as witnesses."

"I know."

"Let's meet at the gas station right here about quarter to twelve." Felipe pointed to a place just north of where they would make the hit.

"At twelve, we'll set up. I'll find some traffic cones and vests. We need to look like part of the construction crew. You'd better get going; we've got about two hours to get ready."

The men shook hands again, and Jorge exited the truck. He turned and faced Felipe before he got in his own vehicle.

"See you there." Felipe nodded and drove out of the parking lot. He saw a crew working on a pothole just a few blocks from the mall and stopped.

"Who's in charge here?"

A beer-bellied man approached the truck and stood by the window. "I am."

Felipe pulled out two hundred dollar bills. "Want to make some easy money?"

Chapter Thirty-Two

"Breaking news in CD Juarez, we will be connecting now with our field reporter, Samuel Velasquez."

"Thanks, Claudia. I am standing in front of a grizzly scene just a few blocks from the American Consulate. Just minutes ago, a commando group attacked an armed convoy that was assigned to protect the newly appointed Director of Security, Antonio Cereceres. Eight federal police, along with the director, were killed in the ambush. Two civilians were taken to the hospital, and their condition is not known. Claudia, the scene here is horrific, like something out of a war movie. The federal police are out in force now, as well as the military, and several helicopters are circling the area looking for the suspects. Witnesses say that there were at least ten men involved in the ambush, and they drove away in two different vehicles directly after the massacre. Police have no suspects in custody and no leads."

"Thank you, Samuel. We'll be back with you when you have new information. Earlier in the day-"

Edilia turned off the television, a look of disgust on her face. When, she thought, would this violence ever end? The President sent an increasing number of troops and federal police, but the situation didn't seem to change.

She turned and caught a glimpse of Saul's desktop in the corner, and for a moment she swore that he was sitting there, as he did many times, typing away some new story, eyes bright with a childlike enjoyment of what he was doing. It was a glimpse of the past, momentarily intertwined with the present within Edilia's mind's eye. It was devastating for her, and her knees went weak as she doubled over with tears and an angry cry boiling from somewhere deep within. She remained there, prostrated, crying unabashedly until her lacrimal glands ran dry. When she looked down, her hands were in tight fists. She opened them and inspected the severe impressions left by her nails in her palms.

Edilia stood and went to the bathroom to wash her face. As she dried her face with a towel, she glanced up at her reflection in the mirror. It was not the Edilia she knew; she was now Edilia the activist, a role that consumed her more than anything she had ever done before. She was too thin, haggard with dark circles under her eyes. She slept poorly when she did actually sleep and ate only when she remembered to, or when Angel would bring something for her when he took a lunch break.

Angel was still doing work on the house, a seemingly never ending project that he continually worked on his days off or when he didn't have any other work to do. She couldn't bear to let him go, and he obviously felt that he still had a debt to pay to Saul. Edilia's cell phone rang. It was Angel.

"Edilia, I am picking up some chicken at El Pollo Feliz. I'll be there in ten minutes, so don't go anywhere."

"I'm not hun - "

Angel had ended the call before she could finish. He already knew her response and was not going to accept no for an answer. Her neighbors gossiped about Angel's constant presence and even made insinuations about their being some kind of a couple, but Edilia silenced them when she said that he was her personal plumber and that she needed his skills every day. Angel arrived right on time, and she let him inside.

They ate in silence, as they usually did, and Angel finished eating most of the chicken by himself. He seemed content that she ate anything at all. Edilia made coffee, and they ate cookies as they sipped on the roasted blend. She felt comfortable with Angel, but she felt nothing else but friendship for the man. Saul was and always would be the love of her life, and no man or any amount of time could change those feelings. Angel seemed very unworried about what she did or didn't feel for him. He ate more cookies in silence.

Long days and eternally longer nights passed. There were actually two days with only one or two homicides, and people actually were pleased. On a Sunday night, Edilia was watching on the news that sixteen young people, including minors, were executed at a party. Edilia sat upright in her chair and took note of the location, Villas de Salvarcar. She got in her car and drove directly to the location. Those people, the mothers, would need her.

Police vehicle's colorful lights marked the area of the terrible scene long before she was even close. When she finally arrived, broken-hearted mothers and fathers were crying as the dead bodies of their children were taken away. Edilia overheard various witnesses and victims narrating and recalling the horrific events. Several men dressed in black paramilitary gear had arrived at the two houses of the party. After one man exclaimed, "Women and children better run!" the men commenced firing. Many ran, but the bullets from the AK-47s were obviously too fast for their escape. The men showed no pity and killed everyone left inside the two houses, including very young girls.

The police immediately branded the massacre as a gang war. Parents defiantly took pictures of their sons and daughters, valedictorians and sportsmen, in their school uniforms, and gave them to the reporters so that they could be highlighted in news programs and newspapers. They weren't, and never have been, gangsters, they indignantly stated. Edilia was empathetic to all of the mothers and helped keep the reporters at bay. She became their spokesperson.

One mother approached Edilia and stood in front of her.

"I know you. They killed your husband, that reporter, right?"

"Yes."

"My boys were killed tonight. My only two boys in the world were murdered tonight. They weren't gangsters. They were in school. They worked to help out with the house expenses. They were good and decent young men, but the police and soldiers are calling this a gang war and saying that my boys were gangsters."

"I know. We won't let them get away with it." Edilia was amazed that the woman wasn't completely overdrawn emotionally.

"How? How do we do that?" Her face bore the weight of hate, anger, and disbelief.

"I don't know. I still have good contacts in the media. We'll figure it out."

Edilia gave the woman her phone number and stayed all night with the friends and family of the victims. Her pain seemed almost trivial compared to the woman who lost her only two sons. Edilia now had a new priority, something even more pressing than avenging Saul's death. Besides, it was all related. The government's supposed war on the drug dealers was the end of the Mexico that she once knew and loved, and it had to be stopped.

Several days later Edilia received a call from Soraya, the mother who had lost her two children in the massacre.

"Did you hear what the President said last night, Edilia? He called my sons gangsters!"

"I heard. I also heard that he will be here next Wednesday."

"I wish I could give that man a piece of my mind. How dare he call those children gangsters!"

"They are trying to make it look like they had it coming, justify it somehow. Soraya, would you really like to talk to the President?"

"I'd like to do more than that. I'd like to strangle him."

"Well, I can't arrange for that, but I think I can get you in at the press conference."

"Seriously? I'd like for him to try to tell me that my dead boys were gangsters to my face."

"I think that having a victim of his war face to face might change his attitude a little."

"You get me in, Edilia, and I'll make him eat his words."

"Count on it. You just be ready."

Edilia called Michelle. "Hi Michelle. I need a favor. A big favor."

Soraya was serious. She had been on television almost every day since the massacre, and her simple yet eloquent speeches were very popular among the people. Edilia picked up Soraya that afternoon to take pictures for their Official Press identifications that Michelle had arranged. All she had to do was get Soraya into the conference. No force of mankind would then be able to stop Soraya from speaking with the President.

The day of the news conference arrived, but as Edilia drove to Soraya's house, she noticed that she was being followed. Judging from its appearance and out of state plates, she reasoned that it was probably a rental car. The car parked down the street and waited while Edilia picked up Soraya at her house. Soraya was obviously nervous, yet very stoic. The car suddenly approached Edilia's vehicle, and Edilia expected that they would be executed at once, so she braced herself. The passenger window rolled down, and a man with dark sunglasses spoke.

"Ladies, this is a bad idea."

Edilia swallowed hard, glad that he was not shooting. Yet. "What idea?"

"You both know what. You are uninvited guests today. It isn't smart."

Soraya sat up in her seat with conviction. "You can tell the President that he can't scare me. I have already had that which was most dear to me taken. Nothing you can do or say can scare me. My life means nothing without them. I'm not going to let their deaths be in vain."

Edilia rolled up her window and sped off.

Reporters swarmed around Edilia and Soraya as they walked to the press conference inside the convention center. The man that had followed them was there too, trying to remain inconspicuous as he continued to follow their every move. Edilia was far beyond nervous, but she had made a commitment to Soraya. Soon, they were past security and in the conference. Edilia knew the most difficult task had been accomplished.

As they arrived, the conference was just beginning. People were still settling in their seats, and there was still just enough disorder for Soraya to make her move. The politicians that sat along the conference tables all rose and clapped as the President arrived and walked to his seat. His wife was already seated, and he took his place beside her.

"Go up there, Soraya. Go up there now and just start talking. Don't stop, and don't let anyone get in your way."

Soraya made her way to the front of the room, directly in front of the President and his wife. She started to tell them that she was the mother of two boys that had been killed in Salvarcar. Reporters that knew who she was began yelling for someone to get her a microphone. The man that had been following them earlier started for her, but the President waved him away. Someone gave her a microphone.

"I wish that I could say that you are welcome here in Juarez, Mr. President, but you are not." She looked at all of the dignitaries. "Forgive me, but none of you are. Since two years ago, terrible murders and atrocities have been committed here, and nobody does anything about it, you know?"

The President merely nodded, his face showing a deep discomfort, as when one is experiencing a sharp chest pain.

Soraya turned to face the crowd of reporters. "But you all clap, oh how great, the President is coming to Juarez. And? That doesn't bring my boys back."

She turned back to the President. "Imagine how I feel. If it had been your children," she pointed at the President, "you wouldn't stop looking for the killers until you had overturned every rock in Mexico. I cannot do that, but you can. Quit talking about it and do something to make this city what it used to be, not the hell that it is now."

Soraya walked away. Everyone stood and clapped. Edilia saw Michelle in the crowd; she was crying, and Edilia couldn't stop her tears from falling either.

Chapter Thirty-Three

Juan stared at the girl on the bus. He had been watching her for weeks. She was barely sixteen, her hair long and flowing, her skin clear, eyes set far apart. She was beautiful. He had staked out her house. Juan had pictures of her house and her family, all in different parts of town. On the backs of the pictures, times and dates were written.

He moved closer to her, and when the old lady that had been sitting by the girl departed the bus, he sat by her. She was texting someone on her cell phone and then looked up at him. He smiled. She looked back at her cell phone without smiling back or saying anything. *That's right you stuck up little bitch,* Juan thought, *in a minute though your whole little saintly attitude is gonna change.* He pulled out the pictures of her family and started looking at them, holding them at an angle so that the girl could see. When she finally did notice and turned to look at the photographs, Juan placed his finger in front of his lips and shook his head. She understood and kept quiet.

"Wouldn't want anything happen to your folks now, would you? They sure seem like nice people."

He shuffled through a few pictures and stopped at a picture of a small girl. "That your little sister?"

She nodded, and her eyes were wide with terror.

"Wouldn't want anything to happen to her, either. You know, there are things a lot worse than death that can happen to little girls."

"Wha-what do you want?"

"Let's get off the bus, baby. That way I can make sure nothing happens to your pretty family. Hey, stop the bus!"

Juan rose and the girl followed him as he casually exited the public transportation, carefully avoiding stepping on anyone's feet. He didn't bother to look back and make sure that she was following; a nice girl like that would do anything to ensure her family's safety. He had been planning this for some time now and had gone over all the possible scenarios in his head. She had no choice but to obey him. They both walked down the stairs that was the exit on the front of the bus. Juan walked with purpose towards his SUV that was parked just a few blocks away, and the terrified girl followed.

"Where are we going?" Her voice was timid, afraid. "Are you going to kill me?

"Of course not. Now don't ask questions. Just follow me and I promise that nothing bad will happen to your little sister or your precious family."

He opened the SUV with his electronic key. The locks popped open, and he opened the door for the girl. She climbed in, her hands trembling. Juan shut the door and walked around the front of the SUV, completely untroubled. He opened the driver door and slid in the seat. They were silent as they drove. Juan was grinning, and his penis was hard as he went over images of himself mistreating the girl and eventually killing her. They stopped in front of an apartment complex.

"You promise that you won't hurt my family?"

"I swear on Jesus' corpse. I won't touch a one of them."

They both exited his SUV, and she followed Juan to an apartment upstairs. He loved the look on her face, like a condemned woman on death row about to be executed, which she was to be, just not quickly. Juan, however, felt as if he were the king of the world. He opened the apartment door and let her in first, pushing her hard as she passed the doorway. The girl fell hard, scraping her knees as she did. She stayed down, and Juan shut the door. Then, turning around, he gave her a swift kick in the stomach, suffocating her.

"Get naked bitch!" He barked the command.

She was crying and trembling, and she fumbled as she removed her clothes, her shaking hands barely able to control her fingers. She kept saying *please, no.* Juan laughed when she did, his answer more cruel than words as he repeatedly beat, raped, and choked her.

Barely an hour passed until the girl finally gave up, the torture too much for her frail body, and she took her last breath. Juan proceeded to poke at her and pull on her breasts, but she did not respond. Juan became disinterested like a child with dead batteries in his toy. He wrapped her in sheets, stuffed her body into a large garbage bag, and carried her corpse down to his SUV. It was dark outside. After shoving the full garbage bag in the back of the vehicle, he lit a cigarette. He felt unsatisfied. *Damn girl died too quick and without a fight. I'll have to pick better next time. All that time and planning for this shit.*

Juan drove the SUV to the outskirts of Juarez in the desert. He removed the bag and dumped the girl's body in between some bushes. The moonlight reflected off the bag. After returning to the Expedition, he drove back to the city. He stopped at a convenience store and grabbed some Tecate beers from refrigerated beverage section. He took the beers to the counter and waited for the clerk to charge him.

"Sorry, no alcoholic beverage after eleven."

Juan smiled and pointed his pistol at the young man. "Make an exception, you fuck."

The clerk reached for the panic button that hung around his neck, but Juan was too fast. He grabbed the clerk with one hand by the string around his neck and dragged him over the counter as his other hand pushed the gun into the clerk's greasy face. The string broke, and Juan threw the panic button as hard as he could. Another man entered the store, and when he saw what was occurring, he turned around and quickly exited the store.

Juan smiled again, thinking about how much he loved this city. He shot the clerk in the head, snatched his beer, and returned to his SUV. He opened a beer and drove to downtown Juarez. He stopped in front of some working girls standing in an alley. One approached the window of the driver's side door.

"Hi handsome."

"How much?"

"Twenty dollars."

"Get in."

The young, thin dark skinned girl obeyed. She pointed to a motel around the corner, and when they arrived, they were given a bar of soap, a condom, and toilet paper at the front desk where a leather-faced old lady charged him five dollars for the room. He paid the hooker twenty dollars when they entered the room.

During sex, Juan thought about the girl whom he had killed and imagined himself strangling her again, as he had done several times before she had died. He enjoyed the thought of taking her to the point of death and then easing up. He never felt so in control. He felt like God.

When he finished, the young whore he was currently with was dead. He hadn't realized that he had been choking her while he was fantasizing. The sheets somewhat wrapped around her head, reminded him of the Virgin Mary.

Juan washed himself with the bar of soap in the sink, and he walked down the hotel stairs and through the lobby. When he passed the front desk, the attendant told him to stop, obviously worried about the girl with whom he had arrived. Juan ignored the man and left the motel.

As he drove away, he finally felt satisfied. But he knew it would be brief. He hadn't snorted cocaine in several weeks. He still drank but no longer in excess. The only thing that he couldn't seem to get enough of was *this*. Every time he killed a girl, the bliss he felt afterward was less and less, that feeling of satisfaction ever fleeting. Soon, he would need to find another girl - another clean, sweet, good, little girl.

Juan decided to cruise downtown Juarez and find a new girl. He liked the preparation involved once he found the right girl - tracking her, taking pictures of her family, and the planning of the abduction. It was better than foreplay.

A girl that looked barely fifteen was waiting for the bus, and he stopped to watch her wait. Juan mentally noted the bus' information that picked her up, and he circled back around in his vehicle. He remained behind the bus, unconcerned with anyone noticing him. He followed the bus until the girl departed, and she walked two more blocks before she arrived at her house. He would have to continue to follow her for the following week, whenever he wasn't working, until he knew her routine and possessed enough pictures to prove to her that he meant business when he finally abducted her. Excited for the new opportunity, Juan pulled out a pair of high-powered binoculars to spy on the girl. A bedroom light appeared towards the back of the residence, and Juan could see the outline of the girl through the closed white curtains.

Through his binoculars, it appeared as if the girl were undressing. Juan fantasized at this thought, but he instead created the scene in his apartment as she was bloody from his punches and trembled with fear. Her lips were swollen, and she smiled as if requesting that he beat her harder, because deep down, she really enjoyed it as well. Juan then decided that maybe he would first dress her like the Virgin Mary, and he became even more aroused.

Chapter Thirty-Four

Ruby had her hair up and wore an incredibly mini-miniskirt and a yellow blouse. She clung to a man at the bar as she flirted hard and whispered in his ear. He was a local politician - the kind of lying and slimy man Felipe would have killed for free, especially after watching him attempt to grope Ruby every five seconds. Felipe found it strangely exciting to watch her bring his prey in for the kill. He thought he might be the luckiest son of a bitch around while knowing that the politician's repugnant hands would never make it past Ruby's clothing.

The politician's bodyguards were busy looking serious and didn't notice Felipe observing them a few tables away. Ruby kept pointing towards a private booth in the back, and when the man finally agreed to go there with her, Felipe made his way towards the dark corner near the booth. The man motioned to his bodyguards that they need not accompany him, and he pulled Ruby by the hand behind him as they walked to the booth. After sitting down, the man immediately started groping Ruby's breasts. Suddenly, Felipe approached and put a bullet in the man's head. Ruby pulled her hair down and removed her blouse to reveal a blue halter top underneath. She then removed her miniskirt to uncover a pair of very small jean shorts.

Hearing gunshots, patrons in the bar began to scream and scramble for the door. The bodyguards attempted to move and assist the politician, but the crowd's collective push was stronger, and the bodyguards were swept outside with the mass of frantic people. Felipe and Ruby mixed in with the panicking people and soon were out of the bar and on the street. The bodyguards never noticed them as they walked quickly to Felipe's pickup. As they left, Felipe noticed that Ruby was panting heavily.

"You okay?"

She smiled and nodded. The night was not cold, but Felipe noticed that Ruby's nipples stood up hard through her halter top. He pressed harder on the gas pedal. After arriving at a motel nearby, Felipe checked in at the front desk and then parked in the mini-garage that was adjacent to their room. Filled with both adrenaline and erotic passion, their clothes practically flew off their bodies and left a trail to the bed.

Later, Felipe watched Ruby sleep. She seemed undisturbed about the murder of the politician a few hours earlier. Felipe turned towards the night table, picked up a pack of cigarettes, removed one and lit it. He, apparently unlike Ruby, was always disturbed by what he had done.

In the city of Juarez, nighttime was rarely silent. Sirens, building and car alarms, and screeching tires often made for a hellish symphony as if composed by some deranged, tone-deaf musician. Felipe was always listening, alert for some tell-tale sound of weapons being prepared for firing, footsteps, or men talking in code. He knew it was only a matter of time before his enemies would send for him. He finally fell asleep, but after a few nightmare-filled hours of restless sleep, he rose at six in the morning.

After Felipe showered and shaved, he awakened Ruby. He watched her flawless twenty year old body walk naked to the bathroom. Ruby always took long showers when time was permitting, so he took advantage of the moment and went through her purse. His mother had always told him never to give a woman all his money or all of his trust. He didn't find anything suspicious or anything that might indicate she had contact with other men. He did find a tiny statue of Saint Death. He had known people that worshipped this gruesome figure of Death herself, the prayer to her just as ominous as the cloaked, skeletal figure.

Suddenly, the ring tone of his cell phone startled him as a kid might be startled by his mother catching him with a hand in the cookie jar. He scrambled to return Ruby's possessions to her purse, and then he answered the phone.

"Felipe, we need to talk. Meet me at the club," Rogelio said directly.

After convincing Ruby to stay at the hotel, Felipe drove to the safe house that was otherwise called "the club." It was just south of Juarez in a small town called Samalayuca, just across the highway from a rock quarry. The military had been recalled from the city, and thousands more federal police replaced the troops. Felipe imagined that it had something to do with what Rogelio needed to talk to him about.

After Felipe travelled twenty minutes on the dusty, gravel road that seemed to lead nowhere, he finally arrived at a gate with a sign, a rooster, a goat and a parakeet painted on it. The club could not be seen from the road. Hundreds of trees and lush vegetation obscured its view, and even the gate was difficult to notice unless one knew it existed. Even less visible were the armed guards perched in the trees with AK-47s aimed and ready to deter any unwanted intruders. Felipe waved to the guards as he approached the gate, and they returned his gesture with a solemn wave that acknowledged his identity and subsequent safety. After Felipe opened the gate, he drove through, got out, and shut the gate behind him. The club had a strict rule of keeping the gate shut, even though it was unlocked.

Felipe parked outside of the huge house that could have been considered a mansion. He approached the door and Rogelio opened it, startling Felipe, although his stoic facial expression did not change. Rogelio's normally happy disposition was displaced by a somberness that Felipe had never before associated with him. After they shook hands, Rogelio waved him inside and closed the door behind him. There were several other men in the room, and Baeza, the boss of La Linea in Chihuahua. Felipe recognized most of the other men as they were all lieutenants in the mafia. They did not rise to greet him or attempt to shake hands, and there were no pleasantries exchanged. Baeza motioned for Felipe to sit. All the men were sitting on plastic chairs that had been formed in a horseshoe; Baeza and Rogelio were seated in the middle. Felipe sat at the only open chair, right at the end of the horseshoe formation. Baeza stood to speak.

"We have been able to infiltrate and manage the military, despite their being under direction of the government and their ties with El Chapo," a look of disgust came about his face as he said the name of his enemy, "and we have been able to get back into the local police, even after they got rid of many of our people. Now the feds are taking over the operation here. I am sure that most of you know what that means."

Baeza looked around at all of the men, ensuring that they acknowledged the extent of their problems. Satisfied, he turned to Rogelio, who stood and began his part of the presentation.

"You are our leadership. I invited Felipe here today because he has become an important asset for our organization, and he will be taking a new role in the company. Felipe, you are now my Captain." Rogelio looked at the other men, anticipating some sort of dis-accord. If there were, no one made it known.

"I have chosen Felipe because he can get the job done. We are still in the business of drugs, make no mistake, but we are also in the business of war. For those of you who have families, I suggest you send them away. This is going to get ugly. We must, at all costs, keep the Plaza. Felipe will be in charge of planning and coordination of all Juarez and Chihuahua hits."

Rogelio placed his hand on Felipe's shoulder. "He will coordinate all of the efforts against the police and main Chapo leaders."

Rogelio removed his hand from Felipe's shoulder and approached another man with tattoos covering all of his exposed skin.

"Chito here, our Captain and leader of Barrio Azteca, will be working along with Felipe, and he will be directly in charge of enforcement and extortion. He is going to put up the mantas, signs on bodies, cut off heads, all that stuff. All of us will have to get our hands dirty, though."

Rogelio walked over to a cooler that was in the corner of the room and dragged it to the center of the horseshoe. Felipe thought he was going to pass out beer and was excited considering how thirsty he suddenly was. However, Rogelio opened the cooler, and instead of beer, there was a man's bloody head on ice. Two of the men sitting nearby nearly jumped out of their seats.

"This is Elvis, some of you remember him, right? Always combing his hair, and those long sideburns." Rogelio shook his head and pointed at the sideburns on the bodiless skull.

"He abandoned us last month when things started getting...difficult. We can't have that. We are soldiers, and this is war. Make no mistake, this-" he pointed to the head, "is the only way out of La Linea. Think of it like a marriage, in good times and bad, until death do us part."

Several of the men squirmed, Rogelio's ploy obviously having served its purpose. Felipe started laughing. The other men looked at him, but he couldn't stop.

"I'm sorry, sorry-" Felipe took a deep breath. "I was just thinking, that has to be the ugliest damn *piñata* I have ever seen."

Rogelio and the rest of the men burst out laughing, too.

"Fuck it, Felipe, I knew you were the right man for the job. Now let's make some *piñatas* out of Chapo's men!"

As everyone left, Rogelio motioned to Chito and Felipe. When they were alone, he had them sit down while he brought a file folder from another room. He opened the folder and handed the men pictures of a woman, a car, the American consulate building, and a house with a spacious back yard.

"I need you two to take care of something this Saturday. This lady is providing Chapo's people with visas to cross to the United States. We have been losing ground in Chihuahua, but it will be harder to control in the States. We need this stopped. This house belongs to a friend of hers. They are having a birthday party for one of their kids. This friend is her contact with Chapo's people. I really don't care about her, just the lady that works at the consulate. The party is at one in the afternoon. Make sure she is dead before she crosses back to the U.S. and don't miss, or we may never have this opportunity again. We have to make a statement to everyone that if you work for El Chapo in Chihuahua, you die."

Felipe and Chito nodded, understanding the importance of the assignment. Rogelio handed them envelopes stuffed with hundred dollar bills. Neither of them counted the money before pocketing the envelopes. Felipe could tell by their thickness that it was a large sum of money.

"Let's have some beer. My captains need to get to know each other. Come on."

Felipe and Chito followed Rogelio to another room in which there were two pool tables, old arcade games, a Foosball table, and an air hockey machine. A large version of a speed bag machine sat in the corner with the title "Test Your Punching Strength." Rogelio noticed that Chito was staring at the machine.

"Go ahead. Try it. I'll give you a hundred bucks if you can hit it harder than me."

Chito nodded and walked to the machine. He attempted five punches and scored the higher end of "Middle Weight."

"What about you, Felipe?"

"I am more of a gun and knife man, Rogelio."

"Fair enough."

Rogelio stepped up to the machine and punched the speed with great power. The machine's bells and whistles were clamorous. The arrow went to the very end of the scoring chart. If he did it to impress the other two men, it worked. He smiled.

"Now, let's play some pool. We are missing something, though, aren't we?"

Rogelio looked at Felipe and Chito as if they were to provide him with the answer to some age-old mystery. Then he nodded and picked up a cell phone that was also a radio. He pressed on a side button, and the familiar beep of the radio echoed throughout the pool room.

"Bring us beer and bitches."

"Understood," said the somber voice at the other end of the radio.

Chito smiled and turned towards Felipe. "That's why he's the boss."

Felipe smiled and nodded. *That, and a thousand other reasons too.* Rogelio was personable, macho, intelligent, and feared. It was a powerful combination, and he was an outstanding leader. Also, he was fiercely loyal to his people, and to Baeza, La Linea's main man in the state of Chihuahua. No one doubted his loyalty, and if Rogelio doubted someone else's loyalty, that person was as good as dead.

When a man arrived with an ice chest, Chito laughed nervously as he wondered whose head was in the chest this time. Instead, the cooler was filled with beer and ice. Several girls arrived much later, heavily perfumed and dressed to please.

Chapter Thirty-Five

Felipe bought the *PM* from a dirty, disheveled man selling the newspaper on the corner at the stoplight. "Three American Consulate Employees Assassinated-Two Year Old Child Survives the Attack" read the headline. Felipe shook his head. It had been a serious cluster. In five minutes he would meet with Rogelio to explain what went wrong. It wasn't so much the fear that Felipe felt about the meeting, but more the apprehension because he hated to have to explain errors, especially ones which were beyond his control. He parked at a seafood restaurant and folded up the paper.

Rogelio greeted him with a handshake, but he was missing his usual smile. The men sat down at a booth where Rogelio had already half eaten a bowl of *birria*, a sort of goat soup, which was still steaming. Felipe declined any food when the waiter arrived at the table to solicit his order, but he did order a beer with *clamato*. The waiter brought a Tecate, *clamato* with shrimp, picante, and lime. Felipe drank some of the beer and poured the rest into the glass with the concoction. Rogelio finished his breakfast without saying a word, and Felipe drank his beer mix. When Rogelio finished, he too ordered a beer.

"Felipe, what the fuck happened?" He said it calmly, without apparent anger. Felipe put down his glass and wiped his mouth with a napkin.

"The plan was to corner the car on the road that led to the Stanton Street Bridge. We were going to flank them on each side. We followed the car from the birthday party, but somehow Chito got behind the wrong damn car. They were similar in color, but different makes. Fucking Chito and his crew were all doped up. Not much else to say, I guess."

Rogelio nodded and then took a drink from his beer. He sat there, without saying a word, as he periodically took drinks from the bottle. Felipe followed suit, not daring to be the one to break the silence. When his beer was gone, Rogelio finally spoke.

"Young man!"

The waiter turned, startled. "Sir?"

"Bring us some more beers! You asleep or what?"

"No sir!"

"Felipe, I haven't talked to Chito yet. He would just lie anyway. I am getting a lot of flack right now because of this. Thank God you didn't kill the kid in the backseat. But Chito's mistake is actually a blessing for us all. The Mexican government will want to appease the *gringos* with an arrest. Let's give them one."

"Chito?" Felipe was surprised by Rogelio's statement.

"Yeah. He is a crappy employee and a dumb ass. I could kill him, but this is better. Gets the government off my ass for this. Pretty sure Chito would prefer jail."

Felipe thought about the dilemma. *Chito would probably be happier to go to jail than die. I would prefer death.* Felipe spent a few years in a Mexico City prison when he was younger. He vowed he never go back.

"Make an anonymous call. The Feds can have Chito and his crew. Give them up."

"Rogelio, I don't want to question your orders, but-"

Rogelio stopped Felipe's statement with a motion of his hand. "I can't trust anyone else to do this. It isn't snitching; it's *strategy*. When it is done, and he is away, you will take over his duties."

The two men drank their beers without saying another word. The Juarez soccer team was playing on TV, losing as usual. Rogelio shook his head in disgust, and Felipe drank more beer. This wasn't his team, so he didn't care. He noticed that Rogelio suddenly wasn't looking at the TV but staring outside. Felipe turned to see Ruby sitting on the hood, dressed erotically.

"Who is that, Felipe?"

Felipe shook his head. "That's my girlfriend. I don't know how she got here, or why. Shit."

Rogelio laughed. "Chicks are crazy. She probably just wanted to make sure you weren't cheating. Bring her on in. I will be leaving in a minute anyway."

Felipe obeyed. He opened the door for Ruby as she walked inside the restaurant. Rogelio stood, as men in old movies always did when women entered the room, and he extended his hand. Ruby grabbed it, and Felipe noticed a strange flicker in her eyes. Rogelio didn't seem to notice.

"Nice to meet you. Felipe has said a lot of good things about you." Ruby smiled.

Felipe couldn't remember ever having mentioned Ruby to Rogelio before, but he was smooth and was probably trying to make Felipe look good in front of her. Rogelio sat with the couple for just a few more minutes, then stood again and said his farewell. Ruby seemed herself again, and Felipe wondered if she had more than a general interest in his boss.

"That guy has a ton of women. Different one every week." He didn't know why he said it and regretted it the moment that he did. Ruby nodded, almost as if saying that she could understand why.

Felipe made the call on his cell phone that Rogelio had ordered him to do, giving just enough information so that it would seal Chito's fate, but not enough to be linked back to Felipe or Rogelio in any way. The police arrested Chito and a few of his crew later that afternoon, and by the following day, the Feds had all of them. Felipe felt strange about the deed, but Rogelio was pleased, so that was all that really mattered.

When Chito appeared a few days later on national news releasing all kinds of information about La Linea, Felipe received a call from Rogelio.

"Go to this Melquidaes Alanis, number 5643, in San Lorenzo. Pick up the old couple there and take them to the club. Chito will shut up soon enough when he knows that we have his parents."

Felipe took Ruby and Jorge with him to kidnap Chito's parents. When they arrived, Felipe, Jorge, and Ruby all exited the truck. Ruby used a small rock to knock on the sliding garage door made of metal bars that stood about seven feet tall like the wall surrounding the house. Felipe and Jorge stood to either side of the door, just out of sight. An old man answered the door without opening it, peering through the metal bars.

"Please sir, help me. Some men just stole my car."

The old man frowned, and against his better judgment, opened the door, a decision he regretted as soon as Felipe and Jorge grabbed and dragged him into the house. His wife was at the door, and Ruby grabbed her by the hand, moving her away from the door so that she could close it. Felipe's plan was to wait until nightfall to transport Chito's parents to the club. Felipe called Rogelio on his cell phone.

"All set."

"Good. Take some pictures and send them to me. Make sure they are tied up and look scared."

Felipe closed his cell phone and turned to Jorge. "Tie the old farts up." Jorge obeyed.

Ruby was in the kitchen, ransacking the refrigerator. She began cooking while Felipe snapped pictures on his cell phone of Chito's parents.

"I think I will rape the old lady when we are done. She isn't that bad." Jorge laughed, the old couple looked petrified, and Felipe's objective was attained.

"Then you can have sloppy seconds." Jorge made a face reflecting his disgust.

Felipe sent the pictures of Chito's parents to Rogelio. The smell of homemade flour tortillas filled the living room, and Felipe walked to the kitchen to investigate the pleasing scent. Ruby had warmed up beans and had tortillas that Chito's mother must have made that morning.

"Look at her! Hottest chick in Juarez, and a good cook to boot!" Ruby smiled at Felipe's compliment.

Felipe remembered the look she had when she met Rogelio, and he shuddered. He would have to keep her away from him at all costs. If she ever left him, he would have to kill her and whoever was with her, too.

"Ruby, I'm going to promote you to lieutenant."

She smiled and laughed. "Sure you are."

Chapter Thirty-Six

"Edilia, what was with all the secrecy the other day? I mean, you showed up here, white as a sheet, and you disappeared for like an entire day. You don't trust me after all we have been through?"

"No, no, nothing like that. I just didn't want to involve you."

"In what?"

"I was at the Mercado, buying cheese and some plant remedies, and I saw..."

Angel waited for Edilia to continue, but she didn't. She had tears in her eyes. "Saw what Edilia?"

"I saw one of the bastards that killed Saul."

Angel gasped. "Are you sure?"

"I'm sure. Do you think I could really forget something like that? Those two men are burned into my memory forever."

Angel thought about it for a while, and then she frowned. "My God, Edilia, what did you *do*?"

"It's better that you don't know. I did something awful. Please don't make me tell you anything more. I'm not proud of what I did."

Edilia's phone rang before Angel could pry any deeper. A deep, masculine voice said, "Stop the march, or you will pay." He hung up.

Edilia had been planning a peaceful march against the military and the Federales for over a month. She had roughly seven thousand people sign up, which meant if she were lucky, half of them would actually show. The protesters would march from downtown Juarez to Zaragoza, the opposite side, blocking all the border crossings to the United States. It was the only way they could get the attention of the people and the government.

Edilia's cell phone beeped to indicate a text message, and after pressing a few keys, she read the message. She deleted the message quickly; it was another threat. She looked over at Angel, who was sitting on the couch, staring at her. He didn't ask her anything, and she figured it was because he already had a good idea of what kind of messages she was receiving and that it would be a waste of breath to try to talk her out of the march. So he gave her a weak smile instead, and she returned it with a nervous one.

"Ready, Angel?"

"I suppose so."

"You don't have to go, Angel. God knows you have already done enough."

"You offend me by even thinking such a thought."

"All right, then. Let's go."

Edilia stopped immediately after saying it and considered briefly cancelling the march. She envisioned packing her clothes and going to El Paso and never looking back at Juarez.

Suddenly, she was struck by memories that drove her purpose. She remembered all of the preparation to gather these few brave people from Juarez - the meetings, the luncheons, and the emails. She thought about Soraya, and her only two children, her sons, bullet ridden and eyes dead to the world all because of a case of mistaken identity. She thought of all the people over the last few years she had met, victims of violent crimes, of the military, of the police, opening their hearts to her, tears pouring, their worst moments relived as they told her their stories. The famous guitarist, all of seventy years old, was killed for a few hundred dollars in his own home. She thought about the man who sold *flautas* and refused to pay "protection" money and the young party people, both men and women, who were killed because they happened to be at the wrong bar at the wrong time. She reflected on the pharmacist who was kidnapped, escaped, and was forced to close his doors forever for fear of retaliation. She remembered the doctor whom she had known all of her life burned to death because he too refused to pay for protection. Numerous young women had just disappeared for no apparent reason, day in and day out, and their parents received no answers from the police. She thought of the men that had been beaten and some even killed, tortured to death by hands of bothtiny voice that they had gained with her support, and hundreds upon hundreds of senseless deaths would forever go un-avenged. She thought about her daughters, whom she only saw now twice a week , her sister raising them for her. She was looked down at the floor, her hands clenched and tears in her eyes.

Angel cleaned the tears with his hands and gave Edilia a strong hug. His compassion possessed no other objective, nothing amorous in any way; it was simply a friend giving another friend simple consolation.

Angel insisted on walking out the front door first. He opened it slightly and peered out, and when he seemingly had made sure that there was no danger, he walked outside. Edilia followed, with much less caution, and locked the door behind her. They walked to her minivan, got in, and she turned the ignition.

The sound of tires squealing from around the corner startled both Angel and Edilia, and they looked in the direction from where the sound had originated. A silver Ford Expedition drove by at an excessive speed above the posted limits, running over a speed bump as if it didn't exist.

Edilia and Angel breathed more easily, and she backed out of the driveway. Edilia drove the speed limit, purposefully taking an indirect route in case they were being followed. A long red light at a corner created anxiety. Men covered in tattoos offered to clean her windows. Another man sold local newspapers, and as he held up the front page, one could read a gory headline with a horrible picture of a headless man. She waved her finger no to the men trying to clean her windshield, and they both retreated, their hollow drug addicts' eyes upon her, the zombies of Juarez.

Edilia and Angel navigated the streets with caution as they attempted to avoid potholes and traffic jams. She still couldn't determine if anyone was following them. They finally reached their destination, a burrito stand near downtown Juarez. As she parked the minivan, Edilia's stomach growled loudly. Angel turned and smiled, seemingly surprised that such a sound could come from this small woman's stomach. They both laughed and exited the minivan.

As Edilia approached the burrito stand, the man making burritos smiled and greeted her. Angel was walking around the front of the van when he felt and heard several fast objects pass by his head.

Dah dah dah; Angel's mind struggled to grasp the events surrounding him, but he recognized the sound made by an AK-47.

Before his eyes, Edilia was hit several times, the bullets penetrating her small frame. She fell to the ground like a puppet that had just had the strings severed, her legs pointing in odd directions, her head forward like a drunkard who had just passed out.

Angel didn't know if shots were still being fired, but he started towards Edilia. He barely noticed the sharp pain and subsequent wet feeling in his back, and he fell down on his face. He was no longer in control of his legs; he willed them to life, but they ignored his commands. He looked up at the lifeless Edilia, and he began to cry. He heard women screaming and the angry voices of men cursing the police, the military, and the government.

People that were to march later with Edilia were arriving. As soon as they saw what had happened to their leader, many of them left in defeat with their shoulders slumped and heads down.

Edilia was dead, and her movement and all of its glory died along with her.

Chapter Thirty-Seven

The girl was tall, maybe five foot nine, slender, with dark, long hair. She reminded Juan of what the Virgin Mary must have looked like at fifteen years of age. She was perfect, and he was excited to know that she was actually thirteen, not fifteen. She was a virgin, and she confirmed her virginity to Juan as he removed her panties to check for himself. The girl was bound by duct tape to a wooden chair, her eyes wide with terror. Her sweat even smelled of fear, further exciting Juan. She was by far the most beautiful girl he had ever seen. He couldn't get over the idea of her looking just like Virgin Mary.

Juan grabbed a white sheet from his bed and tore it in half. The girl trembled violently as he approached her with the sheet, and he placed it around her head, completing the religious appearance. He found it so arousing that he stripped naked. Her already huge eyes somehow opened even more and tears gushed out freely. He grabbed a large hunting knife from the top of the television set and cut the duct tape that bound her feet, and he pulled her up and off the chair. The girl was screaming, but the gag and tape muffled her sound, and to Juan it sounded like a moan of pleasure. He raped her viciously, and while she resisted at first, she struggled less with each slap, jolt, and violent thrust. When Juan ejaculated, the girl was dead. He hadn't noticed, but he had been choking her. He did it again.

"Damn it!" *How dare she die before I could punish her more!*

Juan sat down, staring at the half naked Virgin Mary with her makeshift veil still around her head. He was upset that he hadn't controlled himself longer, but he was still feeling satisfied. He forgave the girl for not living longer.

After he dumped the girl's body out in the Chihuahua desert, Juan took a shower. He was careful not to wash his penis, wanting to preserve her essence on it as long as possible. Juan went to his bed. He had kept her underwear, and he smelled it repeatedly until he fell into a deep sleep, the panties still in hand.

His sleep was interrupted by the music from his cell phone. He answered, "Yeah."

"*Tocayo*! You have a lot of work to do. Meet me at the *office*."

"I'll be there." Juan hung up the phone.

The office was a safe house located in the high-value neighborhood of Juarez. He took a whiff of the panties that were still in his hand, then crumpled them up, and stuffed them under his pillow. He got dressed in jeans, a t-shirt, and tennis shoes, locked his apartment, and got into his SUV. Traffic was minimal, and he arrived at the safe house in only fifteen minutes. Along the way, he had passed by a few traffic cops, but they were either busy or acted as if they hadn't seen him blazing by. They weren't stupid; they knew that stopping certain people could be the last thing that they would do.

Juan drove down the long driveway of the safe house, parked, and exited his vehicle. He knocked on the door three times, paused, then knocked twice more. The door opened slightly at first; then it opened all the way. Juan walked inside, and a man dressed in the garb of cowboy closed the door behind him. Johnny sat at a table, and a young lady was serving him hot tortillas. Johnny smiled at Juan.

"Come have some breakfast. Ana here made tortillas and beans, and there are *chicharrones* to dip into them."

Ana was tall, light-skinned, and attractive, but she was probably in her twenties, so she really was too old for Juan's taste. But, apparently, she was the boss' type as he routinely grabbed her buttocks when she brought food to the table. Ana brought Juan flour tortillas and a bowl of beans to accompany the *chicharrones* and salsa that we already in the middle of the table. She served him coffee. The men didn't talk much while they ate, and after they had finished, Johnny waved the girl away.

"I have a list of people that I need you to take care of right away. Two of them are police that have been working with La Linea for a long time."

Johnny pointed to the first two names on the list which had addresses and phone numbers written beside them. He took a deep breath and then released it slowly.

"Make a statement. Drop the bodies in public places. Burn them alive, cut them up, you know what to do. The others on the list are members of the Aztecas that have been extorting businesses under my protection."

Juan nodded. He knew just what to do, and he would enjoy doing it. He couldn't stop the smile from appearing upon his face, and the boss laughed.

"Jesus, *Tocayo*, you really are a sick bastard. Glad you are on my side."

Juan and his crew spent the next week killing, chopping up, and spreading body parts at schools, parks, and by monuments in Juarez. They taunted La Linea by writing messages on the victims' stomachs, or by taping papers to them with quotes like, "Here lays Seven, right hand man of that fag Rogelio." La Linea followed suit soon after, decapitating some other leaders of Chapo's cartel, hanging their bodies on overpasses with large signs taunting Chapo. It was all a game, and it made Juan laugh.

The murderous game continued for weeks. Juan kidnapped one of La Linea's lieutenants, and La Linea responded quickly by executing several police cadets and a woman investigator that had been recruited by Juan's boss. Juan retaliated by capturing several members of the Aztecas and impaling them on different poles, benches, and other sharp objects in parks and public areas while spreading their remaining body parts everywhere. He smoked crystal methamphetamine, drank, and killed as one day blurred into the next. He felt like a butcher at a meat market.

Johnny sent Juan a picture of a short, plain woman to his cell and then called him. "Her name is Sandra, and she works for La Linea. She collects extortion money from about forty businesses, several of which are under our protection. You'll pick her up and bring her to me."

Juan and his crew waited near the school where Sandra's children attended. She was driving a newer model Chevrolet Silverado, and when they saw her, they blocked her escape with their two different vehicles. Six men armed with AK-47's and pistols ordered her out of the truck.

"Please, please, just leave my children alone!" Tears flowed freely from her brown eyes.

"Just get in the fucking truck!" Juan yelled.

She did, and the two vehicles sped off. The children in the Silverado cried and screamed for their mother.

They arrived at a large house in a fairly marginal neighborhood. It was a house that didn't quite fit in with the surrounding tiny cement buildings. Sandra was blindfolded, and they dragged her out of the truck and into the house. Johnny was at the door with a disconcerted look on his face.

"Take her downstairs."

Johnny's voice was commanding like that of a drill sergeant. Juan had not witnessed this side of his boss. Juan followed the men downstairs where a camera was set up, and hoods were passed out to all the men. Someone wrote on her back with a black marker on her white t-shirt, "I am an extortionist in the service of La Linea."

"Who do you work for?" He yelled, the camera rolling, his voice loud, almost yelling.

"La Linea."

"What do you do for La Linea?"

"I charge the *piso*, protection money for La Linea."

Johnny removed a paper the crew had found in Sandra's purse and displayed it in front of the camera. There was a list of forty-four small businesses with different amounts of money adjacent to their names. Johnny reviewed the names with Sandra, making her confess to her extortionate activities and the amounts she charged these businesses.

"What happens when the people don't pay?"

"They are killed, their businesses are burned down, their family kidnapped. They are decapitated and are made examples of." Her voice was trembling.

"So you are all right with that then? You know that this happens? You know they kill and decapitate people who don't pay? You must be."

"Yes."

Johnny motioned to turn off the camera. He moved close to Juan and whispered.

"Take her and shoot her like the dog she is. And put a rose on her."

Sandra's execution only increased Juan's desire for a new plaything to follow, kidnap, torture, and then murder. After heading to downtown Juarez, Juan found a prospect at a cell phone shop. He saw her from outside the shop, and he followed the girl to various other places in the Mercado. She was like the last girl he killed; she was not quite as tall, but she was easily just as pretty.

Juan followed her all afternoon as he watched her eat, drink, shop, and send text messages on her cell phone. He fantasized about stripping her and putting on the new real veil he had just bought the other day. He thought about the torture, the rape, and wondered what he might do differently this time to this girl.

After the girl boarded a bus, Juan left to get his SUV to follow her. When he arrived at the underground parking lot, a blue Lincoln pulled out quickly from a spot nearby. Four men jumped out with AK-47s in hand and pointed the barrels at him. He expected to be killed immediately and braced himself. One of the men walked closer to Juan and hit him across the forehead with the butt of his weapon, and Juan fell. He then felt hands grab him and thrust him into the four-door truck. The truck's tires squealed as they peeled out of the parking garage. He felt a man's hands bind his own hands with duct tape. The men then bound his head, eyes, and mouth with the tape as well.

Juan fell unconscious.

Chapter Thirty-Eight

The Mexican Army followed the four SUVs over rocky dirt roads deep in the mountains of Chihuahua. The breathtaking and peaceful scenery of green pine trees, streams, and ravines contrasted sharply with the vehicles and the army helicopter that pursued them from above. The men in the trucks fired upon the army vehicles at every opportunity, but the road conditions made it almost impossible for them to actually inflict any damage.

"Son of a bitch, Marcos, I can't hit anyone! The road is too curvy and rocky!" A man named Feo, or ugly, yelled.

Marcos stopped the SUV. "Try it now!"

Feo obeyed and this time managed to wound one of the soldiers in the shoulder. The soldiers responded with return fire and decimated the bullet-proofed vehicle. Marcos was balled up in front of the driver's seat with his 9mm pistol in hand. Feo was dead and so was the young man nicknamed Babyface. Additional soldiers headed towards them from the opposite direction, and soon, the SUVs were surrounded.

The soldiers commenced to fire upon the four SUVs, but the sixteen men were outnumbered by over fifty soldiers. With four men already dead, Marcos and the remaining La Linea members alive surrendered. He removed his button down shirt and then his white undershirt, opened up what was left of the window, and waved the shirt frantically like a white flag in surrender.

The Captain of the troops had his men photograph him with their cell phones as he stood triumphantly over the dead criminals with a victorious smile across his face. The soldiers found C4s in the trucks, along with twelve AK-47s, ten 9mm handguns, three shotguns, and enough ammunition to supply a small army. In addition, they found twenty thousand dollars, although they would report only finding six thousand. They returned to Mexico City with the prisoners and were received like heroes.

Weeks earlier, Felipe had left the old couple at another house guarded by a man and a woman that appeared as if they had not showered in weeks. Chito quit talking to the Feds, but much damage had already been done. Several of La Linea's lieutenants, captains, and their men had been arrested because of Chito's mouth. Rogelio called Felipe to another private meeting.

"Fucking short legs," Rogelio referred to the Chapo, "and fucking Mexican government. Felipe, this is some serious shit. Marcos was arrested yesterday."

Felipe frowned. Marcos was Baeza's son, the accountant for the Cartel in Chihuahua. He handled the payroll and had been really good in the position.

"So does that mean we aren't getting paid?"

Rogelio frowned. "Don't be stupid. I am handling that now. What it means is that we have to put a stop to this right now. We have lost a lot of good people to the police lately. I can't do much with the Army, but I'm working on it. What we can do," - Rogelio made a fist and pounded it on the table that they sat at - "is inspire fear in the hearts of the Feds. I think you know how to do that, but I need you to be very, well, *convincing*."

Felipe nodded. He understood, exactly. Rogelio's cell phone vibrated.

"What? Okay, good, just keep him like that until I get there."

Rogelio hung up and addressed Felipe again. "Let everyone know. Five hundred dollars for every head of any Fed that is brought to me, one thousand dollars for lieutenants and above. I want it to be hunting in Juarez, open season on all federal police!"

Chapter Thirty-Nine

After what seemed like an eternity, someone finally ripped the tape from Juan's eyes. It hurt, but he didn't make a sound. He wasn't about to give these bastards the enjoyment of hearing him whine, scream, or beg for his life. He really couldn't have made much noise, anyway, since his mouth was still covered. Juan was as good as dead, and he knew that it was just a matter of time *before* they killed him, not *if* they killed him.

Juan's vision was blurred from the tape's pressure on his eyes, and when it cleared, he saw a tall, built man standing in front of him. He looked like a *gringo. Have the Americans kidnapped me? No.* Juan saw many Mexicans around, apparently awaiting orders from the American. When the man spoke, his Spanish was so perfect Juan realized that he couldn't be a *gringo.*

"You little piece of shit. You wouldn't believe the luck we had. Or the bad luck you have. I don't care which though," he said, and turned around looking at all in the room, much like a professional speaker would, "because whatever brought you to us, the end result is the same. I do want to tell you, though, how we found out who you were and what you do."

Juan's face was like stone, his eyes brown quartz.

"Hard fucker, huh? A few years ago, maybe you remember this; you and another guy killed a journalist."

Rogelio paused, staring hard at Juan.

"Yeah, I see you do remember. That's good. This is important. See, all of us, and I mean of either cartel, we are all guilty. We are guilty as the Devil, and I have no doubt that we will each have to answer to God or the Devil or somebody at some point. Some more than others, and, well, you have to answer to me, for starters. Anyway, this dead journalist's wife shows up out of nowhere, wanting to set up a hit on one of the sons of a bitches that killed her husband. Normally, I don't handle that kind of thing, but this was different, her husband having been a journalist and all. So I saw her. She had five hundred dollars. I felt sorry for her; I really did. They have some daughters that are orphans now, you know, sad story. So I told her to keep the money and that I would take care of her for free. Like my *penance*."

Rogelio laughed.

"I had you followed for about three weeks. That's how I found out just how sick of a shit you really are. Killing drug dealers, that's one thing, but little girls? You really are a piece of work. Now, I know that you work directly for the Johnny, so you must have some important information. I also know that dealing with a hard mother fucker like you, I will have to play rough right away."

Rogelio motioned to one of his workers, and the man brought a car battery and some cables. Juan knew that the cables were for his testicles. He also knew that his death was going to be a long, drawn out process.

Rogelio tortured Juan for hours as he employed electric shock, toothpicks under the nails, and a hammer. They wrapped a towel around his head and poured water over his face, making him drown without killing him, but Juan never said a word.

When Rogelio pulled out a large Rambo-style knife, Juan recognized it as his own. He figured they must have taken it when they knocked him unconscious. Juan was tired, in pain, and welcomed death. When Rogelio put the knife to his throat, Juan actually smiled.

"I got to admit, you're a tough mother fucker. Not that being tough is going to do you any good now."

Rogelio used the saw side of the knife and began sawing from Juan's throat until he struck bone. Juan no longer saw Rogelio or the other men there; he now saw terrible things all around him - mutilated girls, the girls he had killed, pointing bloody, accusing fingers at him. He felt their eyes staring into his very soul, as his blood ran out of the giant hole he had in his throat. As his head rolled backwards in an impossible angle, for the first time, and the last time, Juan felt fear and remorse.

Rogelio grabbed Juan's head by the hair. "Son of a bitch actually smiled when I cut his throat. Can you guys believe that shit? Armando!"

"Boss?"

"Take this and put it somewhere that all of Chapo's people can see. How about in front of the mayor's house? He seems to like Chapo's people."

"What should we do with the body?"

"Burn it. Burn the whole house down."

Rogelio went to the bathroom and stripped, placing his bloody clothes into a plastic bag. He showered and changed into a fresh set of clothes.

Several men waited for Rogelio to change clothes, gas cans in hand. Within minutes after Rogelio's exit from the house, the entire structure was consumed by a raging fire, the heat unbearable to stand by and watch.

Rogelio had one of his workers drive him to a motel where he had left his parked truck. He walked into his room holding his gun out in front of him just in case. A beautiful young girl was sitting on the bed naked. Rogelio dug through his mind to recall her identity.

"Ruby? Felipe's girl?"

She smiled. "Yes."

"What the fuck are you doing here?"

"I think you know."

"What about Felipe?"

"He doesn't need to know." Ruby rose from the bed and approached Rogelio, pushing away his hand with the gun. She unzipped his pants and got down on her knees. *Fuck it*, Rogelio thought, and then he did.

Later, while lying in bed, Rogelio knew that he couldn't leave things as they were. Ruby was stunning and great in bed, but Felipe was an important element of La Linea's objectives. Rogelio wasn't about to have a problem with him just because of some ambitious bitch's actions. Surely, Rogelio could have just thrown her out, but she would have retaliated in some way as many a scornful woman has, and it would be out of his control. Obviously, this girl had some kind of fantasy that Rogelio would eliminate Felipe so Rogelio could have her to himself. God only knew what her devious little mind had been concocting, but he would not allow for that, or anything else, to happen. He made a plan.

"Ruby, what was this all about?"

"I wanted you from the moment I met you. I had to have you, feel you inside me. And now that I have, I know that I was right."

"So what are you going to tell Felipe?"

"Well, he works for you, right?"

"Yeah, but this is different."

Ruby frowned. "I know. I guess I will just go home and not tell him anything."

"Where does he think you are now?"

"He thinks I am visiting my mother. I was, actually. I just got back."

"How did you know that I was here?"

"I saw you leave your truck here. I was on the bus, and it passed by here at that same moment."

Rogelio nodded. Maybe it was a coincidence, but he really didn't want to know any more. "Ruby, go home with him. Don't tell him a thing. I will deal with it later. Just act natural. I'll call you."

She smiled and gave him a long, passionate kiss. Apparently, it was what she wanted to hear. Rogelio was hard and Ruby took notice; then she took care of the "problem" again. He gave her some money. "Take this, go to the mall, and buy yourself a dress. Go to the mall where the Oaxacans are selling leather goods and handmade goods and buy Felipe some boots or a hat or something."

Ruby smiled and put the money in her purse. When she left, Rogelio did feel a little remorse for what he would have to do, and then he made the call.

"I want to report a woman that is in the mafia. A killer. And she works for La Linea. I can tell you where she will be, what she is wearing, everything...."

Rogelio hung up the phone. He knew that the federal police were working with the Chapo and that they would not arrest her. They would execute her immediately and would ask no questions. It was the only way to deal correctly with this problem. Felipe was far too valuable to the organization to lose him over a girl like Ruby. *She was a great piece of ass though,* he thought.

Rogelio got a call from Felipe. "They killed my Ruby."

"What? Who did?" He feigned surprise, but was actually surprised it happened so quickly.

"That Johnny. Somehow he knew about her, and they shot her like a dog in the parking lot of a mall."

"Damn, Felipe, I suppose we need to take out some sons of bitches, what do you think?"

"I was hoping you'd say that."

Felipe's voice was quiet, low, and probably would have made any other man shiver, but Rogelio smiled. The Ruby incident might have had additional benefits. *What better way to unleash a psycho fucker than by sicking him on the federal police!* They had actually done some damage to his organization and he had to put a stop to it.

"Felipe, meet me at the Papillion. I need to make some plans with you."

Rogelio was already at the bar, and a tall, attractive waitress from Chihuahua served him drinks. He already had gotten her number, and they were planning for a rendezvous after she left work. Felipe arrived an hour later, his eyes bloodshot.

"I made some calls, Felipe. Looks like it was an anonymous call to the Feds that led them to Ruby, but they didn't go as police to arrest her; they went to execute her. She never stood a chance."

Felipe clenched his fists so tightly that his knuckles turned white.

"I have a plan to take out several of them, and I wasn't planning to put you on it, because it is pretty simple, but-"

"I want it. I want anything that involves killing those bastards. Anything."

"Fine. So the first thing that needs to be done is to pick up this mechanic fucker who has been dealing for us. He started buying from Chapo's crew. He has to die, but we can use his ass."

"How?"

"A call to the Feds, a hurt cop, and a bomb."

"I like the plan already."

"Good. My bomb expert will get with you tomorrow. For now, you look like you could use a drink."

"A lot more than one drink."

Rogelio called over to the *mariachis* that were in the corner of the bar. They hurriedly obeyed and prepared to play at his table.

Rogelio picked up his shot glass full of tequila and said, "Salud."

Felipe raised his glass and tipped it to Rogelio's, and they both downed the gold colored liquid. Rogelio told the *mariachis* to sing songs by Vicente Fernandez, and the older *mariachi*, having been around long enough to recognize woman problems of all types, instructed the other to start with "Mujeres Divinas."

The bottle of tequila disappeared, and another soon took its place. The *mariachis'* lead singer's voice became hoarse, but after Rogelio invited the older *mariachi* to join them in drinking a few tequila shots, the lead singer's voice regained its virility, and he belted out a few more songs.

Felipe drank and Rogelio drank. They laughed, and then they became suddenly somber, but neither cried. Too drunk to see the bar-tending girl home, Rogelio said to her that it would just have to be another night because his friend needed him today. She smiled, understanding yet visibly disappointed, or she did a good job looking that way, and Rogelio gave the *mariachis* more money than they had earned in three months.

As the two inebriated men departed, Felipe took the half empty bottle from the table as Rogelio's bodyguards carefully guided them out the door. One of the bodyguards drove Rogelio home while Felipe left of his own accord and somehow safely arrived at a motel.

As Felipe lay in bed, he felt very lonely after having shared a bed with Ruby for nearly two years. *I should have got her out of this after Sandra was killed*, he thought. Alone, lonely, and depressed, he finally cried actual tears. He grabbed the bottle of tequila, drank the remaining alcohol, and passed out.

Chapter Forty

"I still can't believe they got Juan. I thought that he would at least go out in style, guns'a'blazin', taking out cops left and right, or guys from La Linea, I don't know, some kind of grand finale - not just show up one day body burned and head chopped off. First Turco, now Juan, I have to make those sons of bitches pay." Johnny lit a cigarette and dragged on it deeply.

"I have twenty soldiers ready to move." The eyes of the ex-sergeant of the military were cold, dark, and his face was stoic.

"I want you to be creative with the messages to La Linea. Very creative."

"Don't worry. I have lots of practice in killing people. And I make great videos."

"My son is working on that YouTube stuff. Get with him so that he can upload them."

"I will."

Sergeant Zazueta had "retired" early from his military career shortly after a ton of cocaine had disappeared from the evidence building, never to be seen again. It was his initiation into the Gulf cartel, and after two solid years of fighting with the Chapo's group, he decided it would be better to join the competition rather than continually lose against them. He brought his men that served directly under him. They were hit men, and they had been working since for the Chapo in Mexico City, until Johnny called for help.

Zazueta started with various traffic officers that were part of La Linea. He placed their heads on stakes, hanged them from bridges, and burned them alive; it was the usual displays of executed enemies. They stopped at the traffic police roadblocks to steal their weapons and ammunition, a real slap in the face of any cop. Videos on YouTube with titles like, "Cowards of La Linea" and "Dogs, Rats and Members of La Linea" were soon all over the Internet. Zazueta took pictures of his work and sent them to Johnny's son, who then carefully compiled songs available about the Chapo and his leaders, making Zazueta's pictures into a music video of sorts. He ran each attack with detailed plans and military precision.

Zazueta's phone rang. "Z43. Been a long time."

Zazueta smiled, a smile as a shark would have if he could smile. It had been a long time since someone had used his old handle.

"How'd you get this number, pig?"

"Come on, we worked together for how long? You know I have my ways."

"Still running the streets in the DF?"

"Better than that. I'm in charge of the detective department now."

"No shit?"

"Yeah. And I am into something more profitable than the *three animals*." Zazueta understood the meaning of the three animals - cocaine, weed, and meth.

"What could be more profitable than that?"

"You'll see. I'm in Juarez tomorrow. You interested?"

"How long have you known me?" Zazueta said with his shark smile.

Chapter Forty-One

"Kill anyone involved with the Chapo's. Anyone. The men, their women, their children. This guy-" Rogelio pointed at a young man with a camera around his neck and a badge that said "Press" on it, "he is going to film it. I'm not going to let Johnny and his crew continue to humiliate us on the Internet."

Felipe nodded. He was listening, but his brain was on fire with the need for revenge. Ruby was the only woman that he had ever loved. Chapo's men would pay - every one of them.

Felipe and his men waited outside a massage parlor near downtown Juarez. They were waiting for a lieutenant of the federal police. They planned abduct and transport him to another location where they intended to torture and kill him. The young photographer was waiting at the apartment that they had rented the day before specifically for this type of operation.

When the cop finally exited the parlor, he had a smile from ear to ear as he opened the truck door. Felipe's men were behind him, and they pointed their guns at the lieutenant and told him not to move. He obeyed. One of the men searched him and confiscated all the weapons that he had concealed on his person. Felipe drove the van to his men with the middle door wide open. They bound the lieutenant with plastic tie cuffs and threw him in the van, getting in themselves and shutting the door behind them. The operation lasted fewer than fifteen seconds, but they didn't worry about witnesses. Not only was the parlor owned by La Linea, but there was also no one stupid enough to declare himself a witness.

When they arrived at the apartment, the cop was crying, but the duct tape on his mouth muffled his moaning. Felipe shoved him into the living room, and someone shut the door behind the men. He beat the man senseless, kicking him in the stomach, the ribs, the head, and anywhere his foot happened to land. The cop died during the beating. Felipe cut the cop's hands off, almost near the elbows, unaware that the man had already perished.

They drove the dead cop and his hands to the Chamizal, the largest public park in Juarez. Under a giant Mexican flag, they placed the body and set his hands up in front of the body, taping a sign in between them, as if the hands were holding up a sign. The sign read, "He worked for the Chapo." The photographer snapped multiple pictures, one of which ended up in the *PM*.

Soon, a crowd of adults and their children had gathered around the gruesome sight. The police arrived and cordoned the area. Reporters from numerous media outlets assembled at the scene with their cameras photographing from all different angles. The sun was hot, and too many people in the crowd, it felt hotter than ever. Indeed, a hellish burn penetrated the entire area.

Rogelio watched the scene on the local news channel. He drank his coffee and lowered his head. This violence, this crazy war, was not what he had wanted. There had been much more money before the war, before Calderon had taken the presidency. They had all worked together, Rogelio's boss controlling the trade from Mexico City to Juarez. All of Chihuahua had been La Linea's, and for the most part, it had been peaceful. He missed the times when he could go out without bodyguards, pick up girls, and freely spend his money without fear of the other cartels trying to kill him. He still had a lot of money, but he had a harder time spending it. Moreover, he hadn't seen his family since he sent them away to Denver. He had no other choice. No one was safe in Juarez, not even the rich and powerful citizens.

Rogelio sighed, not really wanting to do what he knew he had to do. Three more of his lieutenants and one captain had been arrested. He called Felipe.

"Yeah."

"Felipe, it's time to put the plan into action."

Felipe closed his cell phone without saying anything more. The plan had long since been committed to his memory. After making a few phone calls, he picked up Jorge, and they drove in silence to an auto repair garage.

As they exited the truck, a thick-necked man with an even thicker mustache approached them for service, but Felipe and Jorge were not in need of car repair. Felipe removed his 9mm and shot the man in the gut. The man fell to his knees, ample belly in his hands, blood seeping out. Felipe and Jorge lifted the man, one under each of his shoulders, and they shoved him in the back of the pickup. They drove to a nearby abandoned house and changed the man's clothes for a federal police uniform and shoved him back into the truck. As they drove, Jorge remained in the bed of the truck with the man. Felipe called another man.

"Make the call."

Felipe drove to downtown Juarez in front of the motor vehicle department, slowed, and Jorge tossed the body on the street. Another man parked a Ford Focus on the corner, and Felipe picked him up, and they drove a few blocks away where they could observe the area where they had dumped the body of the dying mechanic dressed as a cop.

Suddenly, two federal police trucks arrived. An older man approached who didn't appear as if he were the police, and after he inspected the body, he attempted to revive the man. Soon after, a reporter and a cameraman from a local news team also arrived. Felipe wanted to wait until more police came, but now there were too many other people, and he knew that even a larger crowd would gather soon. Rogelio didn't like for innocent persons to be hurt, so Felipe called a number on his cell phone, and the Ford Focus on the corner exploded.

Not very satisfied, but with little else he could do, Felipe drove away, leaving his passengers in their perspective dwellings. Dwelling, Felipe thought, because people like them didn't have homes. People like them were condemned men, and they could not know love or the warmth of a family. Nor did they deserve it, as far as he was concerned. He called Rogelio.

"I see it. It is on TV already. It wasn't exactly what I planned, but when do plans go like we want? I'll call you later."

Felipe closed the cell phone and powered it off. He didn't want to talk to Rogelio later or anyone else for that matter. He wanted to drink until he was too drunk to walk, or to stand, or to even crawl, or think. Maybe then he would sleep. He hadn't slept since Ruby had been taken from him. Every time he closed his eyes, the ghosts of his past appeared and taunted him, yelled in their horrendous and dead voices at him, and kept him awake. Ruby had helped to calm these inner demons, but now that she was gone, she had joined the other ghosts and pointed an accusing finger at him. The image of blood gushing eternally from the bullet wounds in her head and chest was still pressing on his mind.

He passed by a convenience store, bought a bottle of Buchanans, drove to a motel, rented a room, and commenced to drink the liquor as if it were water and he was dehydrated. He drank nearly half the bottle within just a few minutes and struggled not to vomit the precious liquor. When the nausea finally passed, he consumed the rest of the bottle. Still conscious, Felipe called room service and ordered another bottle.

Chapter Forty-Two

Rogelio's television blared the live newscast.

"As you can see behind me," the reporter said into the camera, blood on his ear, "a bomb has gone off, and at least three men are dead. Two federal police and another man that happened by were killed in the explosion. The ambulance has been here for a while, and they declared these men dead just a few minutes ago. My cameraman and I were not hurt other than some scratches from flying shrapnel, but the ringing in my ears is terrible."

The reporter stepped aside, and the cameraman filmed the entire scene, moving the camera slowly from the apparent epicenter of the bomb, to the location of the two pickup trucks belonging to the federal police, and to the ambulance. The cameraman panned the camera slower when he passed policemen, their faces haggard and confused.

"There was a car on the corner before the explosion, I am sure, a green Focus. It seems to have been the cause of the explosion. Other than debris, it is gone. As you can see, one of the police vehicles has been severely damaged by the blast, and the motor vehicle department has some minor damage as well. Luckily, there was no one in the building because of the lateness of the day." The reporter walked over to a captain of the federal police.

"Sir, my understanding is that you were responding to an anonymous report of an officer down. Please comment."

"That's right. We were told that a police officer was down; however, I am fairly certain that this was all a setup. No officers had been reported as to having been missing."

"So was this a car bomb or a grenade?"

"As of right now, we don't have enough information. Crime scene investigators are on their way to determine the specifics. My thinking is that the man in uniform was not a real policeman and was maybe either a part of the mafia or another victim. There was another man that came by and told us that he was a doctor, and he gave first aid to the guy in uniform. Those two men and one of my officers are dead. Now I have got to get back to work."

"Thank you, Captain." The reporter turned around and spoke into the camera. "As a matter of fact, and I will need to have this corroborated, I believe the doctor was actually Enrique Palacios, a well-known doctor here in our city. We will have you updated on that and other information as we get it, now, back to you, Marina."

Rogelio turned off the television, not wanting to see any more mayhem that was of his device. *The cop that was dead should have been several, and the doctor, well he should have never been there. That was truly a waste of human life. The federal cops that came down from Mexico City, fucking Chilangos, they deserved to die. When they weren't extorting, they were just downright stealing from people. But the doctor? One that would stop to try to save a fallen Chilango? That was a good man, and he is dead now because of my orders. Another step built in my own stairway to Hell. At least I have the attention of the federal police now,* he thought.

Rogelio picked up his cell phone and dialed.

"Tomas, make a sign and hang it from the Backwards Bridge. It should say that more federal police will fall as long as they work with the Chapo."

Rogelio hung up and yelled to a girl that was in his kitchen preparing some *ceviche*. "Mija, bring me a beer."

A girl around seventeen years of age took him a very cold Indio. Rogelio was normally not into girls that young, but she had thrown herself at him until he could no longer resist. She had a face like an angel and a body that made any man want to sin with her. She was also wise in the ways of the bed well beyond her years. Rogelio slapped her on the rear, and she smiled and blew him a kiss. She returned to the kitchen.

Rogelio opened the beer with a key from his key chain and let it breathe for a few minutes. He drank it, savoring the dark beer's strong bodied taste. *I have to get my mind off of this shit*, he thought, and he gulped the remaining beer. *There is nothing better to get a man's mind straight than a good blow job*, thought Rogelio. He called back the girl from the kitchen.

Chapter Forty-Three

Zazueta smiled and half-hugged his ex-partner in crime. "Fernandez, you fucking pig, you haven't changed a bit."

"You either, you ugly son of a bitch."

The two men laughed and sat down at the table where Fernandez had already been drinking a mixed drink made by Applebee's. The waitress returned, and Zazueta ordered Chivas with mineral water. He remembered what his father used to say, "Only two ways men drink liquor, either straight or with mineral water. Any other way and they are a fag. And never, ever drink from a straw." When the drink was brought to him, Zazueta stirred it a little and then tossed the straw. He drank half of it in one gulp.

Fernandez and Zazueta reminisced briefly about old times in Tepito, a neighborhood in Mexico City known for its high crime and smooth street businessmen. Fernandez had been the watch commander at the time, and Zazueta had made a very dirty cop even dirtier and a lot richer. Working together, they had controlled the streets and all of the criminals in Tepito. No movement was made, no prostitute was paid, no stolen goods or drugs were sold, and no pirating of anything even existed without involving them both. Anyone who defied them met his death. They were two ruthless highly efficient demons streamlining Hell who worked well together. After a few drinks and the small talk, Fernandez, a true salesman, finally got to the pitch.

"So, here's the deal. I have been dealing with some scumbag local police here for a few years, and they have been providing me with *quinceañeras*. The greedy pieces of shit keep upping their prices, though. They know nothing about me, so they have no idea that I'm a cop too, and they try to use that bullshit when I am down here, you know, if I don't pay I can pay a visit to their jail, or their morgue, you know, typical cop bullshit."

Zazueta nodded.

"Anyway, I pay five thousand dollars for every pretty head around that age, or at least looks like they are fifteen. What do you say?"

Zazueta made some calculations in his head. "Make it six thousand a head and I'm in."

Fernandez shook his head and laughed. "As long as that price is frozen, you got a deal. Just one at a time, and make sure they are healthy and no bruises, no cuts, you know, clean merchandise. You know, the drug war has been the best thing to happen for this market."

Zazueta frowned, not seeing how anything was better since the war. "How's that?"

"Before the war, women were getting international attention for their daughters that would go missing. Now with all the people dying every day in Juarez, they can't even keep up with the statistics. Took the pressure right off my little operation."

"I understand now, makes sense. So when do we start?"

"Give me a week or two. I will be in touch. Now one other thing, I pay eight for virgins."

Zazueta smiled his shark smile. "Make it ten and you got a deal."

"Nine."

"Done. Now let's get out of this shit hole and see some naked girls."

"I thought you'd never say that, Zazueta."

Chapter Forty-Four

Ruby was dead. La Linea had been hit hard by attacks both from the federal police and Chapo's men. Felipe had no joy in his life in months. His cousin, Jorge, was arrested for trafficking. He was apparently moonlighting transporting marijuana and cocaine from Cuauhtémoc to Juarez, and he was detained by the military at a checkpoint. His crime carried a mandatory ten years prison sentence, and a shorter sentence would be very costly. Since Jorge was trafficking independently and not doing it directly for the Cartel, he received no help, and the only reason that they didn't kill him was because Felipe had asked Rogelio not to.

Alone in a motel, Felipe hadn't left his room in days, using room service to bring him beer, cigarettes, and occasionally food. Felipe's cell phone rang, probably the thirtieth time since he rented the room, but this time he decided to answer.

"I thought you were dead, *compa*."

"Nope. Nobody's done me the favor yet, Rogelio."

"Shit, don't wish for that, I've already lost a lot of good people. Look, I got a job for you, and I think you are going to enjoy it. And I am still going to pay you well for it."

Felipe looked around his room. He was surrounded by empty beer bottles and discarded packs of cigarettes. He shrugged. "Yeah, why not."

"Meet me at the restaurant. You know, where we first met."

Rogelio hung up and Felipe closed his cell phone. He showered and got dressed, drinking another beer while he did. He reflected on the past few days. He had solicited two prostitutes to his room, and once again, he experienced humiliation when he couldn't perform. He had killed them both and dumped them just south of town. The bitches really shouldn't have laughed at him, not in his present state of mind. He grabbed his belongings and left the room. He would not be back here, not tonight.

Rogelio sat alone at the Chaparral as he drank an Indio beer. Felipe parked and walked to the entrance, looking around for possible ambushes. Rogelio smiled at him when he entered, but Felipe couldn't bring himself to smile. They shook hands and Felipe sat down. Rogelio motioned to the waiter to bring another beer. Felipe was grateful because his buzz was quickly waning, and a headache was taking its place. The waiter brought a beer, and Felipe drank it quickly.

"As you know, Helidoro Silva disappeared after that *Juarez Daily* reporter was shot. Remember the lawyer?"

"How can I forget? He was a pretentious prick."

Rogelio laughed. "Yeah, and I am sure he still is."

Felipe raised his eyebrows. "He's still alive?"

"Unfortunately, yes. He was giving information to the reporter. I never trust lawyers, and when Baeza put me in charge of the Juarez operation, I had him followed. He met with the reporter a few times. I was going to kill the reporter, but the Gente Nueva had him killed first. Silva disappeared the day after. But I know where he is at *right now*. He is visiting his mother in Delicias."

"Tell me you want me to kill him."

"Obviously. I wrote down the directions."

Rogelio pulled a folded up notebook paper from his breast pocket, placed it on the table, and pushed it towards Felipe. Felipe picked it up and stuffed the folded paper in his pocket.

Rogelio continued. "You are to snag him, and take him to the other address that is on the paper I gave you. Make sure he tells you everything about his visits with the reporter. My people there will have video equipment, and they'll take care of the filming."

The men each drank another beer, and Felipe left for Delicias.

The drive from Juarez to Delicias was about five hours. Felipe's only companion was the pack of twelve beers in a cooler on the passenger seat. He passed through both a customs and a military checkpoint as he departed Juarez, and as soon as he cleared the checkpoints, he opened a beer. His buzz remained mild as he drove and drank, and he remained at the speed limit the entire trip. There were still two beers in the cooler when he arrived. Normally, Felipe would hire a gang of *sicarios* to assist him, but he felt that this job would be simple enough. *Fucking lawyers were nothing but highly paid homosexuals in suits, and Silva was no exception*, thought Felipe.

Felipe found the address for Silva's mother, and he parked his truck a few blocks away. His view of the front of the house was unblocked, and there did not appear to be any other exits or entrances to the home except through the front. A newer model Jeep was parked on the street in front of the two storied home. Felipe remembered that the lawyer had always driven a Crown Victoria, but he probably had changed cars. He opened another beer and drank half of it in three swallows. Silva exited the house and got into the Jeep. Felipe choked down the rest of the beer, turned on the truck's ignition, and followed the Jeep for about ten minutes. Silva parked in front of the town plaza and exited. Felipe's recognized his chance, and he removed his pistol.

Suddenly, four federal police trucks, each with approximately six men, arrived and boxed in Felipe. One yelled at Felipe to exit the vehicle with his hands in the air while the others pointed their AR-15s at him. Felipe took a long breath and pushed in the car lighter. He removed the half-empty pack of Marlboros that he kept in his front shirt pocket, chose a cigarette, and then lit it with the car lighter that now glowed red. He took a deep drag and exhaled as nearly fifteen federal police opened fire on his truck.

Chapter Forty-Five

"When can we meet?"

"Tomorrow."

Rogelio reluctantly agreed. "In Acapulco?"

"Yes. When you get in, I'll send for you at the airport."

"Fine."

Rogelio hung up. He knew that he was basically putting himself in the hands of some of the most dangerous people in Mexico, but he had no choice. The Zetas were taking a beating in Nuevo Leon as much as he was in Chihuahua. It only made sense to make an alliance against their common enemy, the Chapo. An alliance with the Zetas was likened to selling one's soul.

After arriving at the airport, Rogelio bought a one way ticket to Acapulco. The next flight out was in an hour. He took no luggage, and he felt naked without a gun. He considered all of the possible scenarios, but the only one he found acceptable was that the leader of the Zetas was trustworthy, they would conclude a deal, and they would be good business partners. La Linea already had a good relationship with the Zetas in Mexico City, so there wasn't reason to believe that they would betray him.

The Zetas smuggled cocaine from South America, through Guatemala, and up to Mexico City. La Linea bought much of that cocaine and smuggled it to Juarez where it was then transported to El Paso and then to major cities all over the United States. The Zetas also distributed the cocaine to the United States, but through southern Texas, and they never crossed each other's territories. The Chapo crossed everyone's territories, and not only was he moving in just about everywhere in the United Sates, but he also was attempting to assume control of the distribution points in Mexico. He was even doing his own smuggling directly from Columbia. Both La Linea and the Zetas had worked with the Chapo in the past, and it had been profitable for everyone involved, but the Chapo became greedy and made his unholy alliance with the government.

Rogelio's plane arrived in Acapulco. As he exited the airport, a short, dark man joined him.

"Need a cab? Number Four is paying for it."

Number Four was the name of Rogelio's Zeta contact. "Yes, I do actually."

The man pointed with his head to a yellow Dodge Stratus with the markings of an airport cab. Rogelio followed him and boarded the car. They did not speak until they arrived at a fancy hotel not too far from the beach.

"Number Four says that a room under the name of Sebastian Gonzalez has been reserved for you, compliments of the Zetas. He'll be in touch tomorrow at 0800 hours."

"Sounds good."

Rogelio stepped out of the taxi. He walked in the lobby and gave the receptionist the name he was told to give, and she gave him a room key without asking for identification. He used the elevator to get to the third floor, and he walked to his room 330.

The room had a king size bed, a small couch and a mini kitchen, and a perfect view of the beach. It was only three in the afternoon, so Rogelio decided to get a cab, buy a pair of swim shorts, and hit the beach. He wouldn't be seeing Number Four until eight in the morning, anyway, *0800 hours, to be exact.* The Zetas were almost entirely comprised of ex-military men, and Rogelio laughed to himself.

Chapter Forty-Six

Rogelio's night was uneventful, although he did end up hiring an expensive hooker for a few hours. His sleep was troubled as he had images of Zeta's beheading people in his dreams. When someone knocked on Rogelio's hotel room door at seven in the morning, he was already awake and just out of the shower. He spoke through the closed door, standing to the side instead of directly in front of it.

"Yes."

"This is your driver for your eight o'clock meeting."

"Give me five minutes."

The taxi driver was the same man who had driven him the day before. They drove for nearly forty minutes. The road was full of sharp curves and lush plants, and trees colored in vibrant greens grew out on the edges of the road. The jungle of the terrain pushed its way forward, seemingly anxious to retake its territory when man's transient stay on earth would finally end.

They arrived at a break in the road where they turned on a dirt road, drove a few more minutes, and then stopped at a guarded gate. The highly armed guards opened the gate and permitted the cab to go through. As they passed, the guards did not attempt to hide their obvious mistrust as they stared at Rogelio. They arrived at the three storied home in a clearing that was barely open in the surrounding dense jungle. The driver turned around to address Rogelio.

"Go ahead, sir."

Rogelio exited the vehicle, and another armed man opened the door to what appeared to be the main entrance. He couldn't help but notice the caged tiger outside at the end of the home. He entered the house into a simple yet obviously expensive living room with a colossal plasma television hanging on the wall.

The five foot eight inch man that stood in front of Rogelio with his hand outstretched did not look like a major player in a drug cartel. His black hair was graying, and his teeth were yellowed from years of smoking while several others were gold plated. His skin was dark. He wore black slacks and a simple off-white *guayabera* shirt. His sandals were of leather and looked to be of high quality and hand-made. Rogelio grasped the other man's hand firmly to return the handshake.

"You northerners are always so damn tall. I'm Nacho."

"Rogelio. Good to meet you."

"Sit down, please." The man motioned to an easy chair as he sat on the couch.

Rogelio saw several pictures on the wall; many of the pictures were photographs that had been enlarged with Nacho in every one. He was dressed in a paramilitary uniform in each, all black, some of him with possible friends or co-workers, others of him with politicians, actors and singers. He was watching Rogelio observe the photographs, and a smirk that appeared on his lips indicated that he was very pleased with himself.

"They recruited me from a small town not far from here when I was just seventeen. I was in the special forces for eight years, and although the training was excellent and I never had any lack for food or shelter, I was always just another *indio*. It didn't matter how much more proficient I was, or smarter, in better shape, I was *indio,* and they even gave me a nickname, *negro*. Funny, too, because it isn't like these guys were light-skinned, tall European types; they were maybe just not as dark as I was. Well, some of them weren't, and maybe they were from the city instead of the country or a village in the jungle somewhere, but we weren't all that different, you know. Yet, I was the *indio*, the *negro*. So when I started with the Zetas, I was happy to see that they didn't give a shit about race or color. All they cared about was results. And now I demand results from those who are under my authority. When I make a deal with someone, I respect that deal, and I expect the same in return."

Nacho stared at Rogelio, perhaps expecting an answer. Rogelio decided to return the stare and say nothing. He would not be intimidated. They both sat for what seemed like an eternity, just staring at each other. Finally, Nacho smiled and broke the silence.

"Shall we get down to business?"

"Thought you would never ask. Basically, I want to strengthen our ties in the United States and increase our forces in the north of Mexico. I need better trained people to combat the military and the federal police. I need some of the prior special forces you have working for you to train and head up some of my operations in Juarez, and in return, I will provide you safe passage and buyers in Arizona, Colorado, Florida, Dallas, Los Angeles, New York, and Illinois. I want to join our resources for both intelligence and manpower in the United States, too. The Chapo has most of Mexico, and he has tremendous power in the States, but his foothold still isn't as strong there, and if we act now, we can control some of that. I have people working on attacking his finances in the States, too, using the DEA and the Feds against him, the few that aren't supporting him already."

Nacho looked impressed. "I have a plan of attack to hurt his resources. We control the Guatemalan corridor. I am looking now at Ecuador, too. He has strong ties in Colombia, but he has to get it here before he can do anything with it. Getting large loads directly from South America to the United States is nearly impossible anymore, so he has no choice but to get it to Mexico first. Right now his strategy is to get the biggest loads by sea to Baja California and from there to California. I am working on ways to stop his sea bound cargo from Colombia to Baja. I like your idea of strengthening our position in the States. If we can control the buyers, we can really hurt his operations. I have a group of thirty elite special forces I can send to you. They'll be on *your* payroll."

"Good. I have a contact in Dallas that can buy three tons of cocaine and ten tons of marijuana every couple of weeks. I supply him already with what I can, but he has been asking for more, so I want you to deal directly with him. We can coordinate pricing so we don't undercut each other."

Nacho was pleased with the partnership, and they spent the rest of the afternoon making detailed plans for distribution, pooling resources, and infiltration of the government in Mexico. After a while, Nacho had a young girl serve them tequilas. As far as they were concerned, the Chapo had the upper hand only momentarily.

Nacho raised his shot glass. "May the next president of Mexico be *our* president."

Rogelio raised his tequila as well, and the shot glasses clinked together. "Salud."

Epilogue

"Your lawyer is working for the Chapo now, Rogelio."

"Figures. Mafia money is hard to say no to."

"What do you want me to do with Silva, then?"

"Make a mess of him and place his body parts somewhere where everyone can see him. Leave a message so people understand he is a traitor to La Linea."

"Understood." Rogelio ended his call on the cell phone with the local head of the Zetas and headed toward the bathroom.

Six months of working with the Zetas had definitely been profitable, but they were a long way from winning the war with the Chapo. They had hit the federal police hard, and now the feds were leaving them alone and going after the kidnappers and extortioners. Cd. Cuauhtemoc, Guerrero, and Guachochi had all been lost to the Chapo, but Rogelio was again in control of those smaller towns. Rogelio observed his haggard face and the deep, dark circles under his eyes as he combed his hair and brushed his teeth. Aligning himself with the most bloodthirsty mafia in the world had definitely aged him.

Rogelio returned to his bedroom. His fifty inch plasma was on mute; the scantily-clad weather girl's mouth was opening and closing making Rogelio think of a fish out of water gulping for air. He slightly turned up the volume, making the sound audible but only being able to understand what was said by straining his ears. He soon fell asleep.

Like most nights, he awoke several times, even the slightest noise bringing him out of whatever dream or nightmare he was experiencing. He finally quit trying to sleep at six in the morning, and he barely raised the volume on his TV. A reporter was in front of the monument to the battle of Sacramento, a battle between Mexicans and Americans that had invaded Chihuahua some hundred and fifty years earlier. The camera was focused on the reporter talking, and what appeared to be a human head was blurred on the screen.

"The head of the deceased is on the steps of the monument, and the rest of the body was spread out on the steps below the head, a sign nearby with a message to rival mafia members. Over three hundred Mexicans died defending Chihuahua against Americans, bloodshed that was courageous and not without purpose. Today's blood is another testament to Calderon's drug war which has directly and indirectly been the cause of over thirty-five thousand Mexican deaths since he took the presidency."

Rogelio laughed. *Fucking reporters*. Even though the area was blurred by the news station, he knew to whom the head belonged. Silva's days as a lawyer were over, unless they had law in Hell, and Felipe's death was avenged. The cell phone rang.

"Rogelio, how are you?"

"Mr. Baeza, it has been a long time."

"Yes, I know. I'm here in Juarez. I need to meet with you."

"Great! Same old place?"

"Yeah, I miss those tacos."

Rogelio headed to the Chaparral. He genuinely was happy to finally see Baeza again. When he arrived, they shook hands and half-hugged and exchanged pleasantries. They ate and drank beer. Baeza was ready to get down to business.

"Rogelio, the Lord of the Skies has spoken with me."

Carrillo-Fuentes had been working underground for so long after his public "death" that Rogelio was shocked to hear Baeza mention him by name.

"He wants to win this war. He's had enough of this shit. I need you to start recruiting soldiers for La Linea in Sinaloa and Sonora. We need to turn this around on him and start fighting at his house, not just at ours."

"How many soldiers do you mean?"

"Thousands."

Rogelio was surprised. "That will take months and a lot of money."

"You have six months and all the money you need. The Chapo doesn't pay his soldiers that well. Triple their pay, recruit people with strong ties to Chihuahua, get policemen, politicians, whatever you can. We need everyone that we can get on our side. We will be quiet for a while, and when we start to attack, we will start in the Chapo's own backyard. This war is going to get a lot bloodier."

Made in the USA
Charleston, SC
06 May 2012